Vole in Paradise

a Sci-Fi Mystery

Thora Wolf

Fall of Rome Books

Empire of Stars and Opals

This is a work of fiction. All of the characters, organizations, and events portrayed in this novel are fictional.

Copyright 2024 by Anna Lisa Loop a.k.a. Thora Wolf

All rights reserved under domestic and international copyright. Outside of the use (such as quoting within a book review), no part of this publication may be reproduced, stored in a retrieval system, or transmitted in any for or by any means, electronic, mechanical, photocopying, recording, or otherwise without the written permission of the publisher.

ISBN: 979-8-9909934-5-7

FALL OF ROME BOOKS

Contents

Chapter One

The Pleasure Planet

V ole Ublion leaned her forehead on the cool of the porthole, cursing Xan again. One of the other passengers muttered something about *selfishness*, but she reckoned he'd quiet again as soon as the entry burn made her position the worst on the transport. She'd gladly trade a fiery atmospheric entry for a few millimeters of personal space. A soft collective gasp signaled they'd entered Bilioth's exosphere.

Ten lurching, free-falling minutes later the ship glided softly over a brown dust planet, the ugliest Vole had seen. She'd only surfaced on a handful since her Combat Medic days, avoiding planetary assignments as much as possible. Her hands clenched their safety loops until her skin paled around the knuckles. Other passengers suddenly seemed huge.

For the tenth time, Vole talked herself out of more meds. She needed to keep her wits sharp, or at least remain conscious. The plan she'd let Xan talk her into was to get acclimated, find Patient Zero, collect the data, and grab the first shuttle home.

Vole pressed her lips together, forcing herself to breathe. Earthen-colored patches passing below brought to mind the reddish pathogen in her MedGen's scopes as they spun up more batches of Alpha polymer, trying to keep up with demand. They'd named the new illness Sairasma. She'd never seen anything mutate so fast, an explosion of cells, living ochre fireworks, a pandemic in the making.

She and Xan needed the one thing humans could no longer have; free access to records. Swallowing her stress, Vole forced herself to look at the faces around her, lives that might be at risk if she failed, mostly young people who had been born during the war. They wouldn't remember things like information sharing, or data collection. They didn't even have trackers.

The ever-larger planet below offered no clues. Its surface presented an impressive collection of domes, ziggurats and odd follies, along with every model of starship half-buried in red grit. Bilioth; pleasure planet for stoned elitists who thought taking insane risks made them enlightened, a playground for eccentric narcissists. *One rotation*, Vole told herself. One night on surface, and then back to work halting the infection.

They landed with a faint thud, taxied briefly, and opened to raw atmosphere freely ionized with stellar dust. Wisdom held you couldn't feel it. But Vole wondered if the electric current in her hair was due to particulates in the rosy air. More likely she was just nervous. Other passengers filed off, carrying survival gear and costumes for their vacations in paradise. But she couldn't move.

"Final stop, Lady," the flight attendant said gently. A middle-aged veteran, gray-haired and scarred, Vole figured he'd seen enough not to judge her.

"Right. I'm going." She didn't.

He peered at her kindly. "When was your last planet run?"

"It's just been a while since I was around so many...people...at one time." Her hand released its hold on a strap.

The attendant kept talking in a soothing voice. "So many civilians, you mean?"

Of course, he'd pegged her as former military, too. She was only two years out of the service and still working at a Command-financed facility. And her bearing probably gave her away as well, how she rarely smiled, and reflexively scanned the horizon for threats.

"I live on Lafford. I'm used to seeing all sorts. Just...not without ceilings...or walls."

"There's been no security breaches on Bilioth, don't worry." He put a gentle hand on her arm, hazel eyes meeting hers. "Give yourself a couple of hours. Grab a drink. By tomorrow, you'll wonder why we don't all live on-surface."

Vole nodded, moving away from his hand, grabbing her bag down from a wire cubby. She could endure touching only with gloves on, and then just for brief moments.

"Of course. Hey, since you work for the spaceline...can you look up someone's address?"

He shook his head, "Nah, rules and regs. Post-war blah blah."

"Right. Uhm, what's the policy about visiting the private side of the spaceport?" She curled her mouth into a smile.

He glanced into the distance. "It's a lawless jungle. If you're looking for a ride to one of the sights, I'd advise you to get an invitation first."

She stepped onto the tarmac. "Thank you."

"Look, ships are going to be all planet-bound until after Solstice. Whoever you're looking for will be here soon, don't worry. Try to have fun looking. Who knows? Maybe you'll find someone better." He winked and closed the hatch.

A flamboyant pink-and-gold sunset played desperately for attention as she crossed to the rustic-chic port building. She followed a few stragglers out onto a staging area, with its deafening warning to naïve visitors not to *step in front of a moving hoverbyl.*

But Vole saw no hoverbyls. All taken, she assumed, by those with the good sense to hurry off the transport. Vole was just about to order a byl on her taeki, when a woman with a stiff maroon mohawk tottered over. She was a stereotypical obnoxious Biliothist, decorated to distraction with adornments, piercings and tats. Her macramé dress clung to her body like shredded cargo webbing, which might have been what it was made of.

"Hi, my name's Minna Tegg. I'll be your driver." Her voice had the resonant rasp of a habitual smoker.

"Oh, good." Vole followed the girl to a dented, dusty byl resting haphazardly in a no-parking zone.

"Just throw your stuff in the back."

Vole climbed into the passenger seat, stowing her bag at her feet. "It's okay. I didn't bring much."

"Not even a coat?" Minna's smile faded. "It gets cold here at night."

"Shouldn't be an issue." In space, the most you needed was a sweater for visiting the observation decks. "I've got a room booked at the Rainbow Bridge."

"Okay." Minna started the engine.

The hoverbyl glided out of the port. According to a compass on the dashboard, their route curved to the south. As they passed cultivated yards and industrial parks, the air switched back and forth between dusty and humid, with a pungent snap that gave Vole the unpleasant sensation of a sneeze that never arrived. She'd been immunized for every conceivable allergen, but the foreign smell didn't help her relax. As they turned onto a ring road, she focused her attention outside, trying not to think about how much she hated planets.

Bilioth from the ground was a parade of odd contraptions and ostentatious facades, punctuated by side swaths of lush greenbelt. Vole wondered if the sculptural shapes she glimpsed in passing had any purpose, or if they were just indulgent follies. As the sky shifted to fuchsia, light ribbons blinked on, revealing vast neon-green jellyfish. They passed into a field that waved like rippling, glowing seaweed, their byl navigating a psychedelic ocean. Vole couldn't resist a smile. Whatever else the pleasure planet purported to be, it was certainly eye-catching.

"Mind if I bubble us? Duskwind is about to kick up."

"Please," Vole said. "Is this whole place art-directed?"

"Only the Playplex. Which is pretty tiny in the grand scheme. Bilioth was reserved for sentient species, you know, when they set up the new rules?"

"But...there must be thousands of people here. All this..." Vole gestured outside.

"Art?" Minna made a quizzical face. "But not permanent housing, see? As long as we live in ships and outbuildings, the Authority leaves us alone. Which is good for you. Since you like to party."

Vole's throat felt dry. "I...like to party?"

"You must." Minna's laugh was a dangerous, low rumble. "You picked one of the funnest lodgings in the plex. The Rainbow Bridge is non-stop."

"Non-stop?" Vole and Xan had chosen the place based on cost.

"Don't let anyone talk you out of watching the marine mammal show. You'll think it's fake, but they actually do..."

Vole interrupted. "Uh...is there any quieter place to stay?"

"Really?" Minna slowed the hoverbyl. "Hmmm...is money a big deal?"

Wind howled outside, pulling streamers violently to the west. The tightness of Vole's skin told her she needed to reduce stimulation. "I'll splurge."

Minna made a U-turn and headed them in the less-traveled direction. They passed several garishly painted terrabyls, three home-made-looking vehicles tricked-out to look like giant animal heads, and a variety of festive kolmis, pedaled up side lanes in groupings of two or three riders. Someone in a transport gave a friendly wave as they navigated around a cluster of the smaller contraptions. Two women with long, wind-blown hair waved back, smiling. Vole breathed slowly and carefully, as a memory surfaced. The last time she had ridden a kolmi was during the war. She'd rolled over a mine, and woken up in the dirt, with stars in her vision, an eye swollen shut, and a broken collar bone.

"No one seems to mind the traffic here," Vole said.

"Nah. This road just goes 'round and 'round. If you want to get someplace fast, best to fly."

After passing a commercial area flanked by monstrous, dancing wind-sock people, the cab pulled off the ring road, crossing a pretty bridge into what Minna called *the Garden District*. The scenery shifted to lush, luxurious estates with wide, closed gates. Gardener Vel.2s worked hanging garlands of tiny white lights.

They slowed, and a pair of gates swung open. At the end of a long alley of trees, the lodging's artful marriage of space cruiser and built structure was seamlessly elegant. Vole swore under her breath. She'd never seen a place so beautiful.

Minna glanced over. "Here we are. Bilioth's boring-est accommodation."

Stepping outside, Vole felt a ripple under her ribcage, excitement mixed with nerves. She steadied herself on the side of the byl, willing herself not to be sick.

"Okay. I'll hover here while you check in. You got plans, right?"

"Not tonight. But before you go," Vole asked, "I'm looking for someone off-grid. Do you have any suggestion for finding someone like that?"

The girl stared. Vole made an apologetic gesture. "Oh, no, nothing illegal. Just, any ideas..."

A luggage Vel.2 approached, holding out rack arms, followed by two security models. "Welcome, guest."

"Gotta go," Minna said, sliding the bubble shut.

The hovercab pulled out from under Vole's hand. "Wait, I haven't paid you..."

"Please allow me to help you with your bags," The Vel.2 said.

"No need." Vole hugged her bag to her body and turned to see the cab's glowing taillights disappearing into the dark.

Xan must have hired the driver as a kindness. Vole's lips pressed into a small smile. He must feel very guilty.

"If you will follow me, valued guest," The Vel.2 chimed.

Twenty minutes later, a concierge Vel.2 flashed one of its hands at a las-lock, leading Vole into a vanilla-scented suite, decorated in creams and blues, with French doors overlooking the grounds and an enormous four-poster bed. Vole could have fit her on-station apartment into the room twice, possibly three times.

The Vel.2 placed a tray on a table and pivoted. "May I further assist you?"

"Nope."

"Medic Ublion," it said, backing toward the door. "You will find services on the interface. Good evening."

Vole found herself blissfully alone. She opened the doors to the gardens, breathing in the green-smelling air. The tray held a large flacon of what turned out to be ale. Vole sipped tentatively, and found its complex bitterness soothed her stomach. She threw herself onto the bed, sinking into its depths, and let out a contented sigh.

Then Vole remembered why she was there and dragged the interface to a coffee table. Its listings contained nothing new or helpful for her search, just ads for restaurants, entertainments, and shops. She put in a call to Xan.

His dark eyes looked tired, but he mustered a bright greeting. "Glad you got there okay. That witch..."

"What?" Vole asked sarcastically. "You mean, esteemed Quadrant Representative Natova Naivos?"

Naivos had been Xan's call of last resort, when they realized only she could authorize a search for Patient Zero. The sooner they got the imperious silver-haired official out of their lives, the better.

He swiveled in his chair to accept something from a MedGen, but kept talking. "She wants me to inform you that our Patient Zero frequents some entertainment palace called *the Aviary*. Maybe he's part owner, or something? Anyway, she commands you to go there. I told her...okay, I insinuated, since she's not a person you can tell things to. I strongly implied that you work for me, and not her."

Vole laughed. Xan normally referred to Vole as his colleague, rather than his subordinate. He understood better than anyone why she had to keep refusing promotions.

"It's somewhere to start. I haven't found anything on this guy that we didn't already know."

He peered at her through the screen. "Are you going to be okay, down there? Looking for...what's Patient Zero's name again?"

"Commander Bo Oliason. I'm fine. I'll be better when we have this situation sorted."

When Oliason had wandered into the clinic a week before, looking like a lost polar bear, Vole had no notion that his case was the tip of a budding pandemic. All she knew was that he was very sick. His entire lower half had been covered in oozing, cracked red skin that he had scratched until it bled. Oliason had admitted he'd been ill for weeks, but thought the thing would go away. Vole had pressed for details, but he had said he was tired and hungry, and needed to grab lodging for the night before all the rooms were gone. Accepting a tube of anti-flam and the assurance that Vole would find a way to help, he had had promised to come back for a blood draw and a debrief, as soon as he had a meal. She hadn't seen him since.

"Oh, that reminds me. Naivos also wanted me to pass on," Xan feigned an arrogant drawl, "*Darling, everyone in the known universe calls the man Oli.*"

"Everyone? How many friends does a merchant ship commander have?" Vole finished the ale, suddenly famished. She opened the lodging interface on her taeki, but the jargon-heavy menu descriptions meant nothing to her. She hit a few items and returned her attention to the call.

"Cargo is only his day job. I'll forward you some journos that Naivos unearthed. Apparently, the guy is a legendary adventurer, what they call a Daredevil. He was a blockade runner during the war. Earned a bunch of medals, I guess."

"Not a selfish jerk?"

"Apparently not."

"I guess he's changed."

Vole lay back, appreciating the watery reflections on her ceiling. If she let her eyes go blurry, with the combination of gravity-legs and rippling lights, she felt she could be at sea. Had she ever been at sea?

"Hello? Are you...enjoying yourself?"

She laughed and sat back up. "Maybe a little bit. Don't worry, I'm not going to come home with feathers for hair and my teeth filed all pointy, spewing about how magical this place is and how evolved I am now."

"I wouldn't care if you did, as long as you get back, sooner rather than later. Two more cases walked in today."

He didn't need to explain to her how he felt about telling people that the rash on their genitals would soon turn to crusting sores, giving way to high fever and rupturing lymph nodes. With a polymer injection, they had a good chance of recovery, though they didn't yet know how good. Vole had personally examined seventy-seven cases. Of those, sixteen had died. All of them had spent time on Bilioth.

Her doorbell chimed.

"You have a visitor?" Xan sounded hopeful.

"Just dinner. I'll call you tomorrow."

A Vel.2 rolled in a table and with a flourish, uncovered a sumptuous array of foods. Vole didn't know what anything was called, but it was all insanely delicious. Full but unable to resist, she devoured two miniature pies smothered in cream, decorated with sugared pink blossoms. Her stomach groaned.

Vole pushed the rolling table out into the hall and slammed the door, guilt stricken, then sank to her knees. She had eaten much more than need required. Her blood pressure spiked, a flush rising up her skin. Had her gluttony resulted in hunger for someone else? She knew that the world was no longer in the throes of famine, but taking more than your share was still a sin. Wasn't it? She sat and looked around the lodging, disoriented. The place was too nice, with its soft bedding and sweet-scented air. Why was she there?

Panic throbbed with Vole's heartbeat, signaling an impending attack of tremors, then the horrors that followed. Vole laughed bitterly, congratulating herself that she'd managed to last almost three hours on-planet before melting down. Finding her satchel, she downed a dose of meds. Then she flipped through the articles Xan had sent, waiting for the rush of calm as the chemicals did their work.

Pictures popped into her taeki; Oliason, in his glory days, a handsome, well-spoken man of forty. He seemed to have visited every developed planet and many still wild ones and bragged shamelessly about all the pleasures he'd consumed while exploring so many untamed frontiers. Vole sighed. There were hundreds of places he could have picked up an infection. According to Naivos, he'd gone straight from the Waystation clinic to Bilioth. What was so important here, that a man would risk his life?

Numbness washed over her. Her brain functioned, now separated from her body, perfectly rational. Her vital signs normalized as the sense of immediate doom dissipated, leaving only an exhausted void. She washed and went to bed.

Wind ruffled the trees outside, and shadowy blobs danced on the ceiling, everything pinkened by solar particles. There was something oddly soothing about the glow that complimented the med-induced fuzz in her brain. Vole liked the way the lodging's thick coverings hugged her, dragging her forcefully down, into sleep.

She dreamed that the transport she'd taken to Bilioth was burning, and falling, and that everyone aboard was screaming.

In the dream, all she felt was relief.

Chapter Two

Minna

Vole woke confused about her whereabouts, remembering slowly that she was on a planet, and alive. Birds whistled in the trees. The sun was high in a rosy sky strewn with lazy lavender clouds. She rose from a sweat-soaked bed, washed and dressed, and ordered a hoverbyl to the Aviary. The room's interface informed her that the club would be open in eight hours; *could she be persuaded to take in any of a provided list of Bilioth's attractions?*

"No," she said.

She fell back on her bed, considering. "Good Ship. Do you loan out kolmis?"

The kolmi shed was past a merry manmade brook swimming with neon-colored coy. The immense fish followed Vole, making ripples in the black water, which roiled and glittered under a curved metal bridge.

"Find someone else," she said to them. "I didn't come here to feed genetic experiments."

They disappeared.

"I'm sorry," Vole sighed. "Are you...sentient?"

The brook lay still, like a glass snake fringed by reeds. She found *the Shed*, a barn-like building lined with sporting equipment; boards of every description, myriad small boats, and a neat row of colorful three-wheeled kolmis. Vole flashed her retina and picked out a gold-glitter model, with fat tires and a skull-shaped hood ornament. It was the least flashy.

Vole sat and began pedaling, rolling along a smooth, empty path that hugged the brook. Cool air in her face distracted her from the fear in her stomach. But within five minutes, all she felt was pleasure. The path crossed onto another resort, and then another, each starship-bunker surrounded by lush gardens designed according to some theme Vole didn't know enough to identify. Most places had fruit and vegetable gardens, and pens with pretty livestock. The message seemed to be that if war returned, the people on Bilioth could ride it out in comfort, and if the going got really tough, they would fly away.

The place certainly aced the self-delusion game.

In an hour Vole, frustrated that all she had seen were other tourists and other resorts, arrived back at the Good Ship. The Shed's interface lavishly praised her *athletic prowess*. Vole laughed out loud.

Her taeki chimed. *I'm in the driveway.*

Vole headed through reception. Today, Minna wore a jumpsuit of green scales, and elbow gloves. Vole had on the only clothes she had brought; a beige coverall.

"I forgot to thank Medic Aizmirst for hiring you. But this is so thoughtful."

Minna donned a pair of glamorous sunglasses. "Isn't it?"

Hovering onto the ring road, it was clear Vole was the only person on Bilioth not wearing tough leathers or oddly cut confections of silk and ribbon. The whole place was out of a synth game. People pretending to be avatars.

"Thank you for the suggestion on the lodging. It is quiet." She glanced at the cab's time display. "Where are you taking me, now? Xan didn't inform me."

"I'm not surprised." Minna laughed. "You're looking for Oli, aren't you?"

Of course, Xan would have told her that much. "Do you know where to find him? I was going to try this place called the Aviary, but it's closed until evening."

"They open at dusk. Unless you're the sort who plays day games."

"What are day games?"

"If you have to ask, never mind." Minna glared. "Surely you know Oli's preferences, though? What he gets up to?"

"Not really." Vole blinked. "So, you know Commander Oliason?"

Minna laughed. "Duh."

"Good," Vole said sharply. "I really need to talk to him."

"No kidding," Minna said sarcastically, speeding up the cab. Buildings and parks raced past.

"Could you please slow down?" Vole felt a shift in the atmosphere, as they left other vehicles behind. "Where are we going? And why do we have to get there so fast?"

The byl sped up even more.

"I'm the one who has questions," Minna rasped. "For instance, who is Oli to you?"

Vole gripped her seat, her gut stirring uneasily. "Why don't we grab a cup of tea somewhere?"

They had entered another district, this one landscaped with shapes that might have been trees or sculptures, their blood red shadows whizzing by.

"Maybe, if you tell me where he is." Minna cranked the cab to the left.

"Minna," Vole spoke in her best bedside voice. "We need to slow down."

The cab started to wheeze. "Who told you he's at the Aviary?"

"Pull over."

"Answer me. Who's he with?"

Vole reached over and closed Minna's nostrils with her left hand, pulling the emergency lever with her right. The girl whirled on her, scratching with long, sharp talons.

"I disabled that lever. Do you think I'm crazy?"

The cab listed as they turned into a black tunnel. Vole's voice echoed in the frigid air. "What's going on?"

"You tell me." There was a sound of gravel spraying.

The tunnel opened to a bridge. Vole tried to see ahead. She felt for her safety belt, but the force of her angle made it impossible to unlatch. "I can't help you unless you explain what's wrong."

"Where is Oli?"

"I don't know. That's why I came all the way down here. Let's work together, how about that?"

The cab began to whine as Minna turned them down a dirt road leading through scrubby land. Another hoverbyl approached in the opposite direction. The driver motioned helplessly as they rushed toward him.

Minna moved controls, causing the byl to lurch upward. It shimmied, trying to hover higher, but something was wrong. The floor pounded sickeningly, engines straining. Panic showed on the other driver's face as he passed below them, barely clearing their byl.

"Stupid tourist," Minna growled. "Wish I had hit you."

"I want to find Oliason, too," Vole said calmly. "I really do, but this isn't the way."

"Oh, and you know everything? Your ugly clothes, your pasty space skin, and those death eyes." Rage seeped through her words. "I guess you're the one flavor Oli hasn't had."

"I'm the what...?" Vole's words were cut off by a horrible, deafening sound of tearing metal.

She was spinning free, wind hitting her skin, and a smell of something base, like rust. Fear blossomed inside her like a stain. She pressed her eyes shut, body clenching automatically into the crash position.

Vole sailed through cool, dry air, scraping her shins on the ground as she skidded, and came to a stop. Then the only motion was her stomach roiling, the only sound a tick of cooling metal. She opened her eyes. Her seat console was planted in the dirt, near the edge of a gulley made of reddish clay spiked with tall grass. The place had the feel of a back passage in an off-season zoo, littered with smoking shrapnel that had once been Minna's hoverbyl.

The soldier in Vole took firm control, the mechanism in her that knew what to do when someone was broken and bleeding. Unlatching her safety harness, she grabbed her bag and ran, falling and sliding on loose debris, scraping her shins and ankles. But the pain felt muffled, as if it were happening to someone far away.

She found Minna between some rocks, glassy-eyed, skin gray and sweaty. Vole sent a distress call.

"Internal injuries. Shock," Vole said, taking Minna's vitals. The girl muttered incoherently about Oli, and how he needed to know what was coming.

"Don't fight me." Vole moved Minna into the recovery position. "Help is coming." The girl whimpered in pain and pushed Vole's hands away.

"You'll need to tell them what drugs you're on."

Minna's voice was thick with tears. "I'm not on anything, dumb-ass."

"Then why were you driving like that?"

"To scare you into telling me where Oli..." Her eyes rolled back in her head.

Emergency Services consisted of two commercial MedGens who hastily loaded Minna onto an ambubyl. They checked Vole's vitals, ignoring her explanations, and sprayed her cuts. Then they glided away.

"What? You're just leaving me here?"

Silence. Vole pulled up a map on her taeki, tracing the road the MedGens had taken, which ended at a hexagon where the eight district pie slices converged, labeled *Vortex Park*. It was encircled by the ring road, with a Medotel icon on the northernmost point. Vole had heard of Vortex Park. It was the location of the annual Solstice Fest, an event notorious diaspora-wide for its life-threatening performance injuries and quest-drug overdoses. Good place for a Medotel.

Shouldering her satchel, Vole began to walk. She couldn't help squishing ant-like bugs and centipedes on the rough gravel road. Vole thought about the neon carp, and wished she knew more about the fauna of Bilioth. Were the centipedes sentient? Was she committing a crime by killing them? It occurred to her that they were drawn to the scent of blood from her cuts, and might be trying to feed off her.

A driverless hovercab eased next to Vole, with a comforting, mechanical hum, sliding open its door with a rush of air conditioning. Her left shoulder blade was starting to ache from the crash, and dehydration had started pulling subtle threads in her head.

She flopped gracelessly onto a seat. "What a relief. How did you know I was here?"

The interface said in a soothing voice, "I was summoned by Emergency Services. Would you like to go to the Medotel?"

She checked herself. "No. Take me someplace to eat. Near the Aviary."

Chapter Three

The Aviary

They left the dirt road down a narrow alley. After a quarter of an hour the byl merged onto a bustling street. More people in superfluous gear and artful costumes. Should Vole know what characters they were emulating, or were they simply heroes of their own pleasure games? A woman passed by on a hovercycle, what appeared to be a large dog in goggles sitting placidly in the side byl.

Vole blinked. "That was a dog, right?"

"Please rephrase the question."

"Never mind. What district is this?"

"Ologidisi, Madame. Here is a restaurant near the Aviary, as requested."

Vole stepped out in front of a chrome-striped facade with a sign spelling out the word HOME. Across the street stood a swag-festooned mansion that recalled an old-fashioned cake. Two long legged metal birds, beaks fused together in a kiss, topped a weathervane, which twitched nervously in the pink sky. The Aviary. The place looked deserted.

A service Vel.2 showed Vole to a table. The room was huge, sparkling clean, and nearly empty. A menu appeared on the Vel.2's tablet, but she had no energy to lift her hand and peruse it.

"Would you like to start with a cocktail, Madame?"

She scanned. "No. Maybe. What time is it?"

"Our soup of the day is..."

"It's okay. Just bring me your three most popular items."

She made a noise of frustration. No response from Oli on her taeki, and no mail from Xan. Vole's brow furrowed, as she checked to make sure the thing was working right. It was.

"Our most popular items, Madame."

The Vel.2 set down a tureen of soup, a slice of colorfully iced cake, and a bottle of sparkling wine.

Vole reached for a spoon, wincing as an electric ache ran up her arm, to the top of her head. "Do you have any ice packs?"

"Ice packs? I'm sorry, I don't understand. We have ice. We have iced tea. We have iced..."

"No. What about cold packs? First aid?"

"Aid? Lemonade? Would you like to see the menu?"

"No. You can go." She waved it off.

The soup, thick with marrow and vegetables, warmed Vole's body with alarming intimacy. She scraped her bowl, then ate all the cake, forcing herself to taste its delicate combination of sweet, light, and crunchy. One glass of the tingly wine sent delicious fog into her aches. Trying not to think about the cost of her meal, she sat gazing numbly across the street.

The Aviary's weathervane shifted prettily. People shuffled through the gate and down a side passage. What were *day games?*

"They're strict about no spectators until duskwind, I'm afraid," came a folksy voice from behind her. "Shouldn't sell out, though, so you're fine. The Solstice crowds won't be here for a few days, yet."

"I need a ticket?" Electric shocks ran down her left side as she twisted. A man of around fifty, with a braided white beard and beringed knuckles shot her a craggy smile.

"The restaurant sells 'em for cash. If you don't want your business tracked." He winked.

"Cash?" Vole laughed. "That's a good one."

"Of course. Cash is an archaic notion from the ancient past."

Vole paused. He was serious. "Biliothists mistrust the Authority that much?"

"Completely." He shrugged. "You disagree?"

She smiled. "Not really. Would you...care to join me, Sir?"

"I thought you'd never ask." He slid in across from her and held out a spangled hand. "Name's Nyppio."

"Vole." His fingers enveloped hers in dry warmth. She pulled away.

"You're new here."

"I'm a tourist. Which...you already knew, since you offered me such kind advice."

Nyppio half smiled. "Of course."

"You sound doubtful."

"Not at all. What else could you be?" He gazed hopefully at the wine bottle.

Vole signaled for a clean glass. Nyppio explained that all citizens of the Playplex started as tourists. "And then we couldn't leave."

"Why not?"

He laughed delightedly. "You'll see, my dear. The Aviary is a perfect place to start."

"Do you know..." She took a shot in the dark. "...Commander Bo Oliason? By any chance?"

Nyppio's face sobered. "Of course, most everyone does. Why do you ask?"

Vole shrugged. "I can't really address that."

"Ah. You an investigator?" he said lightly. "Not that I'd stop liking you. But are you?"

"Why would you ask that?" She poured wine.

"You're sniffing around for Oli, a man many people are looking for."

"Many people are looking for him?"

Nyppio laughed. "He has an intoxicating effect on women. And business associates. And the Daredevils. They hate to love him, of course. But he's their elder statesman."

"Why is he so important?"

"Why were the astronauts who traversed Phrast Nebula heroes? Or the team that sent humans down Morpho's Hole?" Nyppio imitated an Auth-Prop narrator. "Explorers on the vanguard of our nation; risking their lives for the human diaspora."

"Sorry to be so ignorant. But how is Commander Oliason an explorer on the...what was it you said?"

"Now, Vole. You must already know that, seeing as you're staking out his night club." Nyppio downed the wine and rose. "Nice to make your acquaintance. I'd offer to tell Oli he has a stalker, but that'd be like warning a rose bush about the bees."

He strode away, pulling a hood over his white hair.

"Anything more, Madame?" asked the Vel.2.

Vole ordered tea and wrote a message to Xan, leaving out the accident. He must be counting the hours until she solved their riddle of the illness. She closed her eyes, breathing slowly, tucking the med cannister deeper into her bag. She counted to ten, and then backward from ten, and then...she was floating in a dark, earth-smelling place, and she ought to escape before it closed her in...

"Madame, will there be anything further?"

She started, awake. The fuchsia sky told her hours had passed. Streamers and flags flapped frantically in the wind.

"I'm afraid there is now a wait for tables. If you are not eating, kindly make room for others."

"Of course. Sorry." She went to the restroom and splashed water on her face. The circles under her eyes looked flatter than usual, and her cheeks were pink from the morning sun.

The air outside had cooled. Pairs of streetlights popped on as Vole crossed the road to the Aviary, following a stream of people down a side path leading to an old-fashioned conservatory. Its myriad glass panes within arching metal frames reflected maroon sky, like a vast gem. She scanned in at a door.

"Medic, you are a new guest to us. Welcome," purred the entry interface.

"I'm looking for Bo Oliason. Is he here?"

"Your purchase is complete. Please enter."

"May I speak to someone in management?"

"I cannot find any information about your question. Please enter."

A line had formed behind her. Vole stepped onto a polished stone walkway winding through trees, their branches thick with tiny, colorful birds that flitted and preened. She followed a couple of men down through the green canopy. A Vel.2 stood in a doorway, observing with its unblinking, electric blue eye.

"I need to speak to management."

"I'm afraid I have no information about your question. Please find your seat. The show will begin presently."

She spoke slowly. "Supervisor."

"I'm afraid..."

"Boss."

"I'm afraid..."

"Dammit, I need to speak to a person. A live person."

Other people passed them. The Vel.2 pointed one of its many arms. "I'm afraid I have no information about your question. Please sit. The show will begin presently."

"You will report my presence to management."

The Vel.2 didn't move.

"All right. I'll find my seat."

Her box was near the top of a steeply raked cylinder lined with other such cubicles. A rope bridge connected tall wooden doors on opposite sides of the chasm.

Vole sat forward in her seat, looking for an interface. Before she could ask for anything, the lights went down, and a spotlight appeared. One of the wooden doors slid open.

Chapter Four

Banned for Life

Chapter 4, Banned for Life

"Medic, do you require Emergency Services?" The interface said calmly. "Are you in distress?"

"Tell them to let me loose."

The two security Vel.2s released her. She stood stiffly in the side passage outside The Aviary, brushing dirt off her sleeve from where she'd fallen into a flower bed. Security disappeared back inside, and the door snapped shut as if reprimanding her.

"I need to speak to a person. A human person." Her voice shook.

A trio of Biliothists strutted drunkenly to the entrance, flashed their retinas and disappeared inside.

"The Aviary guarantees satisfaction." The voice was infuriatingly even. "You have been issued a full refund."

"Too late. Can't un-see that."

"I am sorry to inform you, but in future you will be denied entry to the Aviary. Thank you for your visit."

She couldn't stop herself from yelling. "I am a Command Medic, and I have permission from Quadrant Representative Natova Naivos to make inquiries about one of your investors."

The blue eye stared straight ahead.

"Record a message for management. I need to speak to them. They can find me at the Good Ship."

Vole hustled back out to the street and waded into foot traffic. The Aviary's weathervane spun merrily. She hugged her light coverall around her against the cool duskwind. It took several minutes of desperate gesticulating to get an autobyl. People called out to her in passing, inviting her to come along with them and party. One man told her not to cry.

"I don't cry, civilian," she muttered, then cursed under her breath. She was a civilian, too, now.

The vast, glistening byl that pulled up next to her was intended for a group of eight. Two men in passing kolmis smiled up, asking if she was *all good?* She jumped inside the byl and called out instructions, then sucked down one of the small bottles of whiskey from the mini bar. As they left the cloaked zone, her taeki pinged. Three messages from Xan.

"Dammit!" She swore to herself. Xan, who had no idea how handsome his dimples made him during staff meetings when he joked about their diminishing resource list. Xan, who expected her on the evening shuttle.

Vole blinked, wishing for the millionth time in her life that memory was linear, and erased parts could be restored, while things like the Aviary show could be deleted. Of course, people had always had sex with animals. But as far as she knew, never while actually flying. She lay back, sipping her second whiskey. She liked the taste of it, its smoky sweetness. Horrible as the show had been...the chemical reactions inside the brain must be startlingly vivid, for the rare man who could stay on his bird. Her science mind contemplated Oli's past presence at the place, his reputation for adventure.

"Ugh," She grunted. "I'm not sure I want to know where he got sick."

Vole sent Xan a message stating simply that she was making progress. But she'd need to remain on Bilioth for one more day. Then the whiskey kicked in.

Chapter Five

Birdland

Vole woke to a flawlessly pink dawn. The Good Ship's complimentary breakfast, served in a restaurant-bar off the lobby, made her eyes water with pleasure. She mopped up the last crumbs, watching out the window as brightly colored monkeys gamboled in the trees outside her room. She was about to try and talk to them when her taeki buzzed. Xan.

Naivos is getting frustrated.

Vole replied: *Naivos can come find Oliason herself, if she thought it was so easy. And by the way, where is the Med data waiver the politician had promised?* Realizing she was venting, Vole rephrased the message to be more diplomatic. Xan had enough on his plate. They agreed she would check in that afternoon, when she had tracked down her only lead.

Vole stood outside the lodging boutique for a long time, working up the courage to enter. She'd never needed shimmering dresses, tailored leathers, or any of the other attention-grabbing items on offer. But both Nyppio and Minna had insinuated that Vole's coveralls broadcast her employment in a way that didn't help the cause. She entered tentatively.

"Just browsing," she said to the Vel.2 .

"Very good, Madame." The robot was a glamorous monster; human-form on top, with a reptilian lower half.

The array of choices made Vole uncomfortable, their many colors and textures, each fine and functional, each terrifyingly expensive. She rarely needed to buy anything on-station, and saved almost all of her salary. But the reflex to deny herself was strong, the sense that she'd need her credits in some cataclysmic future. Who was she kidding? The human race wouldn't survive another large-scale disaster. A jeweled orange button flashed up at her. For some reason, Vole couldn't look away from its fiery depths.

"May I help you?" The Vel.2 said.

Vole started. "Please. I need a new outfit. Something that says, *I belong here.*"

"Very good." The Vel.2 circled Vole, its electric blue eyes moving over her body dispassionately.

"I have assembled three ensembles in your size. Would you like to try them?"

"Oh." Vole considered how long it would take her to decide something so ephemeral. "No. I'll take the least expensive one. I also need a coat."

"This rounder offers five in your size."

The Vel.2 motioned to a rack of sumptuous garments. Vole grabbed a puffy, russet parka with a fur-lined hood. "This looks warm."

"It can be compacted."

The Vel.2 stuffed the jacket into its own pocket, then closed the packet. Vole crammed it into her bag.

"The pants and tunic you have selected will adapt to extremes of temperature and humidity. They were created for..."

"Show me where to change."

Vole was pleased at how unfamiliar she appeared in the slim, russet leggings and a long, close-fitting indigo tunic. Her heart-shaped face and short, dark hair seemed less severe against the rich colors the Vel.2 had picked out.

"I'll take this water bottle, too."

"The water is complimentary, Madame."

"You're well programmed."

The Vel.2 bowed at the waist.

Vole left her coverall in the equipment shed and borrowed the fat-tired gold kolmi. After a wrong turn, she found Minna's route from the day before; the tunnel, the bridge, then the gully where Minna's byl had crashed. Scorch marks were all that remained on the dirt and grasses. The road grew rougher as she reached the edge of the Playplex. The only living beings seemed to be lizards, though they skittered away so quickly she couldn't be sure. A blanket of red grit inched up equipment and outbuildings, spraying under her three fat tires.

The border itself was nothing more than a shredding metal fence with a faded placard; *proceed at your own risk*. Vole left the kolmi next to a cluster of tractors and began walking. She felt light and free, then immediately guilty for forgetting the gravity of her task.

Cottony clouds striated the pink sky, shading darker toward the horizon, where solar dust shimmered. A strange delirium hovered in Vole's chest, causing her to sigh contentedly. Maybe it was a delayed reaction to the accident, or maybe it was the overwhelming presence of life all around her, so different from being in space. Flowers grew abundantly under her path, their tiny yellow blossoms surprisingly tender. Small shrubs were camouflaged with silvery scales. And what a beautiful spider, its furry white legs gently brushing her hands, large chelicerae moving in to bite.

Vole snapped back to awareness, brushing the arachnid to the ground. She tucked her hands in her pockets and hurried away. She had heard stories of people going mad on Bilioth, eating or drinking chemically altered substances they then couldn't purge. The air was warming. She took a sip from her water.

She was thinking about the virus, its' symmetrical, precise structures and accelerated growth pattern, when Vole's foot struck a low wall marking the entrance to *Jaisenet Nature Preserve*. She hobbled inside, trying to avoid putting weight on her throbbing left toes. The landscape began to shade more bisque than ochre, and vast shards of gray granite loomed thirty or more meters high, like gigantic loaves of half-buried stone bread.

Shadow passed over Vole, a solitary Jaisenet gliding overhead, silhouetted black against rose. Her breath caught in awe. Vole hadn't gotten a proper look at them during the show, distracted by the drunk, naked men trying fruitlessly to pull themselves onto the birds' backs. The Jaisenet, now gleaming teal and bottle-green, alighted soundlessly in her path. It was almost twice her height, though much of that was neck and legs. The creature cocked its head appraisingly, looking her up and down with an emerald eye.

The bird squawked, beckoning with its shiny green-black bill.

"Hello." Vol scrambled after it. "I was hoping to speak to one of your leaders."

The Jaisenet began a slow, graceful walk deeper into the refuge, checking every few steps to make sure Vole was following. It led her through dry creek beds flecked with spongy, yellow-green shrubs, and thick forests of stone. Vole called after it again, but it ignored her. She scrambled on.

They reached a brown-rock seam with a sheltering crevasse just wide enough for them to pass through. Here the bird stopped, its eyes meeting hers.

It clicked softly. "Tck. Tck."

"What is it? You want me to follow you down there? Is there someone I can speak with?"

The bird's legs were as high as Vole's shoulders, its haunches quadruple her width, though how much was muscle and how much feathers, she couldn't say. Something about its proud bearing and complicated coloring made Vole think of the bird as female. Her magnificent, feathered train hovered millimeters over the stony ground, without once brushing it.

The creature motioned with her beak and repeated the clicking sound.

"Okay," Vole said, and the bird walked into the passageway. It was shaded, but dry, lined in packed gravel that made no sound under the bird's splayed feet. Vole tried to be quiet, but her footfalls echoed around them. In five minutes, she walked out to a wide, gravel clearing amidst more granite formations. It smelled like rock dust, and greenery, though Vole saw nothing growing. She was beginning to feel dizzy, probably from dehydration, but she didn't want to drink all her water until she knew how long it would take to return to the lodging.

"Could you...give me some indication of where you're taking me?"

The bird swished its train behind it and turned to the left, walking swiftly.

"Okay." Vole's boots made a hollow sound as she stepped forward a few paces. But something felt horribly wrong. Her stomach lurched with fear. *Where had the horizon gone?*

Empty space opened up around Vole's body. She was falling into nothingness, into a depthless vault of air and light. Her mouth opened to scream, but then her tunic stretched tight onto her body, and she was wrenched backward, coming to rest at the edge of a wide cliff. Vole fell to her knees, gasping for breath and blinking back tears of panic.

The blue-and-green bird loudly reprimanded with a series of clicks and squawks. Vole stared up at its wide, teal breast, her nerves flaring with seismic urgency. A hard beak pressed her further onto the cliffside plateau.

"Sorry," Vole squeaked, crab-walking away from the edge. "I didn't see..."

Noise shattered the air, a thousand bird voices echoing her guide's. Vole reflexively moved to cower behind a boulder, bracing herself. The cacophony softened at the sight of her distress. She gulped, steadying herself for the panic her body was sure to lock onto now, the chasm of angst she would fall into if she failed to take meds. But to her amazement there was no residual flight urge. Aside from some faint soreness in her toes, Vole felt fine.

"Thank you." Vole shouted. "I'm okay now."

The avian chatter moved on to what she sensed were more interesting topics. The blue-and-green bird's eye led Vole's attention to a crease in the cliff's uneven face, where a rope railing was tied to a stout iron loop. A hood appeared, then a woman alighted. She was tall and slender, slightly bent with age, her robes well-made and clean. She held an ornate metal and wood walking stick, which gave her the air of a druid.

Blue eyes met Vole's. "Come with me before you kill yourself."

Vole knew the voice from recordings and films.

"Scientist Arpina Karpolo? I'm so very glad to see you."

Suddenly, the air was alive with the pounding of wings. Fifty or more birds circled out over the valley, gliding on a downdraft, eight-meter wingspans glinting like a colorful nebula.

"I'm sure you are," Karpolo sniffed. "Did no one tell you this planet is full of dangers?"

Arpina Karpolo turned and disappeared back the way she had come.

"Am I supposed to follow you?"

Vole stepped to the cliff edge, where the rope handrail continued beside a set of steps carved into the cliffside, just wide enough for one person. Karpolo was halfway down.

"Sure. I'll be right there." Vole muttered to herself, gripping the rough rope until it dug into her hands, trying not to look out at the valley. In the hazy distance, she got an impression of rolling, golden hills with copses of leafless trees, and reflective black lakes.

Vole breathed, focused on the nesting ground as it came into view. Birds of many vivid colorways groomed one another, chattering conversationally in a low rumble. They swooped out dramatically into the air or landed gracefully on the white-stained edges of caves. Some held their wings out to the sun like bright fans. In the shadows stood spindly juveniles, their molting feathers like piles of dirty cobwebs obscuring patches of jewel brightness. They seemed to be watching her.

Finally, Vole stepped onto a wide span of level ground beneath a half dome of rock, excavation marks visible on its high ceiling. The scooped-out piece, clearly manmade, was as big as a space station. Dripping, vine-draped walls sheltered a graceful, old-fashioned villa overlooking the valley.

"This way, Command Medic."

"You...know who I am?" Naivos must have alerted local functionaries. Vole didn't dare check her taeki to see if Xan had sent news of the data waiver, for risk of being rude.

"You've not exactly kept a low profile," the old woman said tartly. "Never mind. You'll take a cup of tea before you leave. Just to make sure you don't kill yourself accidentally. People become lightheaded in this climate."

"Yes, Scientist."

Vole found the Villa's shining wood floors, crystal chandeliers and decorative millwork charming. Once inside, Karpolo lowered her hood, revealing a gray braid, a sun-brown visage dominated by a sharp nose, and penetrating blue eyes. Two shaggy young men greeting them by waving rubber-gloved hands. Karpolo introduced them as her research assistants and ordered them to bring tea. Vole couldn't see what they were doing, but a familiar chemical smell told her it was specimen related.

"In my office." Karpolo led Vole into a room full of untold wealth in the form of books, which lined every wall, and glimmering, antique-looking instruments in glass cases. The place smelled like wax, dust, and a pleasing tinge of old wood.

"Thank you so much for speaking with me, Scientist. I studied your work at the academy. Your discoveries are groundbreaking."

"Is that what you've been told?" Karpolo motioned for Vole to sit. "How very odd. Command doesn't acknowledge my work with grants, or awards. Only by making me famous amongst...clinicians."

Vole smiled at the reference to the now-archaic tension between medics and scientists. "I understand your time is valuable. So, I won't waste it with small talk. I'm looking for a pathogen."

Karpolo spoke with condescension. "So sorry, but you *are* wasting my time. My birds are perfectly healthy."

Her birds? "Do you know anything about Commander Bo Oliason?"

"Hmmm. Probably nothing out of the ordinary."

"I'm under orders from Quadrant Representative Naivos. As I'm sure you understand, I can't elaborate." Vole needed to be careful. Finding Oliason would mean little if she lost her license. "Commander Oliason is not under criminal investigation, if that worries you."

"No one worries about Oli, pathogen or no," Karpolo scowled. "I am surprised you're not trying to arrest him for cruelty to animals."

Vole felt her eyes widen. "I have no jurisdiction to arrest anyone, Scientist."

"It was a joke." Karpolo smiled absently. "You're not the first young woman who has come here trying to find Oli. Though some of the other girls are, not to offend, but, a bit more glamorous, perhaps?"

"Let me guess," Vole said, "the last one had a mohawk, and a tooth jewel, and appeared to be on the verge of overdosing?"

Karpolo folded her hands in front of her. "Sounds about right. I don't remember that much detail. Only that she was hell bent on finding Oli. She had a different story about her reasons, of course. Almost as flimsy as your own."

One of the research assistants entered with two steaming mugs on a tray. He set them down on the desk, then disappeared. It seemed to Vole that he avoided eye contact.

"Scientist. I really need to know. Where is he?"

Karpolo sat back, blowing on her tea. "How should I know? Drink up. You're dehydrated. No doubt that's why you keep asking the same question over and over."

"Thank you. A cup of tea sounds lovely." Rude patients were often hiding something, waiting for just the right question to reveal it.

Vole picked up the bitter-smelling mug and studied the cluttered room with its thick, patterned rug. Karpolo had obviously been on Bilioth for many years, since before the Playplex. Since before the war. No doubt she had waited out the entire Vel.1 uprising here, where work was done by humans, and she was never in danger of mechanical servants.

"I'm grateful to you for pointing out my weakness as an investigator. Do you have any advice for a younger person of science? A lead, a suggestion? A further critique of my methods?" Vole pretended to sip the tea. It burned her top lip.

"All I have is common sense, which you apparently lack." Karpolo cocked an eye. "It seems obvious that Oli doesn't want to be found. Clearly, the Authority have tried..."

"Scientist. Commander Oliason made me a promise to meet and speak, and I must hold him to his promise. It's a matter of clinical importance." Vole met the older woman's eyes, which remained impassive. She kept talking, improvising, pretending to make a difficult decision. "And... critical importance, for my research. Give me something. Please. I can offer you co-author credit on the paper."

Karpolo's eyes gleamed. "Would you, now?"

Vole allowed herself the slightest glimmer of sorrow.

"If it meant we would be published. I would personally deliver the drafts for you to edit, of course."

"You're really desperate." Karpolo's deep voice dropped to a whisper.

Vole kept her expression neutral. "I am."

"I don't need you to collaborate with, you impertinent brat. But, if it will get you to leave here and allow me to do my work, I can offer at least some context."

"Thank you."

Karpolo removed the cloth cover from a tall, hand-sized bronze object, a cross between an animal skeleton and a leaping water droplet. "Have you ever seen one of these?"

"No. Should I have?" Vole stared.

"It's the Universal Award for Daring, the AUD. Only a handful of men have ever attained it. One was my son." Karpolo's face grew strained. "Who died soon after."

"I'm so sorry." Vole rarely felt surprised about people's confessed losses, and Karpolo didn't strike her as maternal. "Your son was a Daredevil?"

Karpolo nodded, expressionless. "Sharm Karpolo. He was on Oli's team. Half the idiots who come to this planet are dreaming of this trophy. They all want to find Oli, either to beg him for a spot or to sabotage him."

"My reason for coming has nothing to do with..." Vole gestured to the trophy. "The AUD."

"Of course it does. The Playplex only exists so idiotic young people can test themselves. Top Daredevils are legendary." She waved her arm. "All over the diaspora."

"This practice of bird mounting..." Vole said softly. She still felt ill at the thought of it. "Oli..."

Karpolo rolled her eyes. "He wasn't the first to accomplish it, of course. But his prowess is...well known. For a big man, he's quite graceful."

"May I?" Vole touched the trophy. She'd never seen anything so ugly. "Tell me about the Jaisenet birds, Scientist. If you wouldn't mind. Open my provincial, space-centric mind."

"You're actually rather clever, Medic." Karpolo laughed, then started hacking. "Not at all what I was expecting."

"Someone told you to expect me?"

Karpolo made a derisive face. "The birds did, obviously. Gossip has it you were poking around the Aviary."

"The...birds?" She smiled.

"You're surprised I speak their language?" Karpolo puffed.

"Yes, as a matter of fact. It's...very impressive." She barely kept her mouth from turning up, into a smile.

"They noticed your evident concern for their wellbeing. And they were amused also, by your naivete."

"Do they understand what the show...what...the show is?" Vole flushed.

"Of course. They're very intelligent. But the touch they experience isn't as depraved as it looks." She leaned toward Vole. "It doesn't hurt. The Daredevils aren't animals, just stupid youngsters with too much energy, and no war to fight..."

Vole sensed the old woman drifting as she sipped her tea. She pretended to sip hers, smiling. "Might I ask them where Oliason is?"

"Absolutely not." The old woman let out her breath impatiently.

"Do you ever visit the Aviary?"

"Never," Karpolo spat. "But I consult with their trainer. The birds they use are still part of this flock, you see. I have known them since they were hatched."

"In your opinion, are they...slaves?" Slavery was a serious crime.

"No. They go of their own free will. They have their reasons."

"Reasons?"

Karpolo clicked her tongue. "You think only humans can make rational decisions? The Jaisenets are sentient. I have been working with them for thirty years. I know everything about them. And they are doing fine."

"So, no leads on Oliason? None?"

"It occurs to me that you need to get to the top of those stairs before the sun goes down."

Vole felt woozy. How long had she been there? She looked at the deep brown liquid in her cup and realized that Karpolo believed she'd drunk it. Was the old woman trying to murder her?

"Yes. I should go."

Scaling the steps was easier than descending them had been.

When she got to the top, Vole looked around, but the only birds she could see were in flight, or inside their shadowy caves across a narrow strip of dropping-bleached ground she had no desire to cross.

Down the passage between the forest of stone loaves, Vole caught a flash of pewter in the corner of her eye.

"Hello?" She hastened to the clearing.

Standing by the entrance like a sentry, a magnificent, silver-graphite-pewter Jaisenet preened itself with a lustrous black beak. It stopped and regarded Vole with jasper-red eyes, nostrils flaring.

"Hello." Vole dipped her body into an awkward bow. "My name is Vole Ublion."

The bird shook its tail feathers, then dipped its large body, its black tail feathers elevating in a proud semi-circle, casting a filigreed shadow.

"Oh, my. You are...magnificent."

The bird relaxed back into a normal posture with a soft swish. "Jauhuaa."

"What?"

It repeated the sound and flicked its eyes skyward.

"Jauhaa," Vole repeated. "That's someone's name?"

The bird flicked its eyes again, as a violet-lavender-rust Jaisenet alighted on a pile of boulders a few meters away.

"Jauhaa," the pewter birds said.

Vole bit back a smile. "Thank you. And your name...?"

"Karr'a'a'a'a."

"Thank you for your help, Karr'a'a'a'a. Greetings, Jauhaa." Vole bowed again, moving between the birds, facing Jauhaa. "I wish to ask the whereabouts of a man named Commander Bo Oliason. They call him Oli?"

Jauhaa tipped her head to one side, then the other, listening. Atop her head, a deep ochre coxcomb rose, and her bill emitted a series of soft purring sounds.

"I've come a very long way to speak to him. It is important."

The bird croaked, not unkindly.

"Jauhaa?" Vole looked at the bird. "Has Scientist Karpolo told you that the humans are sick? That if we don't find out where this illness is coming from, some, in fact probably many, will die?"

Behind her, Karr'a'a'a'a screeched, scratching the valley floor with one long, sharp talon. The great bird tipped her beak skyward and let out a long series of burbles. Vole recognized it as a crude imitation of human laughter.

"Jauhaa, can you help me?"

Both birds rose off the ground with a rush of air, as if frightened. Vole heard the sound of angry yelling from down the short trail, at the cliff edge. Karpolo. She hurried back out the way she had come, as cawing birds circled in the pink air.

Chapter Six

Plunging In

By the time Vole had trudged back to the Playplex, she had finished her water, her skin itched from dirt and sun, and the gold kolmi was gone. She cursed and called Xan, relieved when he didn't answer. He wouldn't approve of her staying another night. Her voice wavered as she lied on a message that she had a good lead on Oliason.

Shadows were long when she arrived at the Good Ship, and the wind had begun to stir. She flipped through the interface's dinner menu. Her fingers stopped at an image of a vast, pale-blue mineral pool.

Vole picked out the most modest swim skin in the boutique, iridescent white, and still far too revealing. She shrugged. It would be dark soon. She ate a quick plate of local game and vegetables, all delicious, and hurried to change.

The ice-blue water of the mineral pool was soft with dissolved salts and clouds of air bubbles, everything shades of aquamarine and mauve under the deep-pink dusk sky. Vole star-fished face up, ears warm and muffled, weightless. Although she had taken no meds, and probably had little of them left in her system by now, she felt calm. She ought to be biting her nails to the quick, the way Xan probably was.

But there was no sting to the guilt Vole felt. It had been a long day, and she was too tired to wonder why her body was cooperating with her plans, for once. On-station, her fits often inserted themselves between her and her patients. Between her and Xan, who couldn't even comfort her with a soft touch. She was pretty sure he wanted to, though.

Xan once said she would be running the whole quadrant's clinics, if not for her affliction. He was being kind. The truth was, a less patient supervisor would have let her go ages before. He insisted that her trauma-sickness helped make her a better medic. He couldn't hide his worry about what would become of her without Lafford Waystation clinic.

Maybe she could just float, forever. Vole paddled around a bit, seeking the cooler and warmer places. Far off in the distance, a flock of birds undulated like a living cloud, a reverse nebula, dots of darker sky that grew and compacted, swooped and whirled.

Vole felt lightheaded. The scent of tiny pastel flowers which had grown in sandy swaths beneath her feet tickled in her nose, pungently sweet. Vole sneezed, then laughed, feeling ridiculously out of place in her expensive swim skin, which was cut for someone much more comfortable with their body than she was. Someone without so many scars, Vole thought, meaning almost everyone.

She pulled her left leg out of the pool. This one was more disfigured than the right, though either one frightened onlookers. She stretched, studying her limb as she would a stranger's. Pain, not too bad most days. Function, normal enough. Cosmetically unacceptable, but expensive to fix. Liquid sluiced down the deep, vertical crevasses in her skin. Were the Biliothists' markings a fashionable way to cover their own scars? Replacing her limb in liquid, Vole gave thanks for the fact that she had legs at all, when many veterans had had theirs blown clean off.

Vole's scars predated the war, though trauma-suppression protocols had removed their source from her memory. She'd made up a story to tell anyone who asked, that she'd gotten caught in a harvester working in fields as a child. But no one ever asked, because no one ever saw.

Sweetly singing amphibians serenading her from the black lava pool edge. *Eck, eck, eck.* The flower smell seemed to grow stronger, and with it a feeling of wellbeing that pushed away all troubling thoughts. Vole was beginning to suspect the pollen had some medicinal properties. It might be worth sampling them, to see if they had use as a sedative. Bilioth might have some value, after all.

Saffron wavelets of cloud crept across the fuchsia sky.

"Madame, may I offer you a refresher?" A service Vel.2 wheeled over with a tray in two of its eight arms. The machine looked strange in the pool's underwater lights, like a cartoon villain, the tiny blue light of its eye bright against the darkening shrubs. "I have several flavor profiles available."

"Oh, so glad you popped up." Vole felt sudden energy. "I need information. Can you tell me where Bo Oliason is?"

There was a short pause. "We have no one registered under that name. Perhaps a different name?"

"Xan Aizmirst?" She tried the next name she thought of, as a control.

"I'm sorry, we have no one registered under that name. Perhaps a different name?"

"Do you know where I can find the hoverbyl driver, first name Minna, last name Tegg?"

"I'm sorry, there is no registered hoverbyl driver, first name Minna, last name Tegg."

Vole tried alternate names for Oliason, but none registered. She asked who the owner of the Aviary was, but that information was unavailable. She asked where Bilioth's Medotel could be found, but visiting hours were over. The Vel.2 sent the address to her taeki.

Scooting to the side of the pool so she could see the Vel.2's interface tablet, she asked for local journos with pictures of Oliason. But the ones that popped up told her nothing new. There were shots of the tall, handsome man competing in various physical competitions; spelunking into a cave, rappelling down a cliff, and gliding in a flying suit, arms outstretched like marsupial. How ironic if what killed him was a disease. There were several images of AUD Champions in a row, smiling.

She slipped back into the water, letting it cover her shoulders. "Tell me about the Universal Award for Daring."

"The Universal Award for Daring, also called the AUD, is a non-monetary prize given to the top Daredevil each year on planet Bilioth. The five most recent winners are Bo Oliason, Sharm Karpolo, Devon Kristenhaim, Drew Manchap, and Calest Michellonu. The competition is held annually, with a different series of challenges each year."

"When is this year's competition?"

"It was held two months ago, and the Champion was Calest Michellonu."

"Was there a Jaisenet Bird component to the prize this year?"

"This year the competition consisted of climbing Mount Grakkikik, spelunking the caves at Mon-mon, riding a Chartreuse Serpent, wind sailing from the Airy Spire to the Black Crag, and taking a Frou-frou in the Bangoo Grass Desert."

"What is a Frou-frou?"

"A Frou-frou is a sex worker who specializes in a kind of play acting designed to create the illusion of..."

Vole interrupted "What is the point of the AUD competition, if not a money prize?"

"Champions are awarded a trophy."

"So. Glory? Immortality? Everyone knowing you can take a Frou-frou in the Bangoo Grass?"

"I'm sorry. I'm afraid I don't understand."

"Never mind. Where is Bo Oliason?"

"We have no one registered under that name. Perhaps a different name?"

"I mean on Bilioth. Where is he?"

"I'm afraid the Proclamation of Peace specifically prohibits the sharing of location information, as well as all records, communications, and collected data, unless necessary for Authority functions."

She sighed. "I had to try. Where do the Daredevils like to hang out?"

"I have sent a list of equipment suppliers, camping grounds, and public parks."

She ran a hand through her wet hair. There had to be a faster way to locate Oliason than loitering in shops and parks.

"Where do the Daredevils practice?"

"I have sent a list of climbing walls, snow caves, and a local night club called the Aviary."

Vole paused. "What would you do if you were trying to find a person on Bilioth, and you didn't know where to start?"

"Call them."

She'd called Oliason fifteen times. "What else?"

"Message them."

She'd messaged him twenty times. "Do you have any other ideas for me?"

"I have many ideas for you. There are several entertainments I can suggest. I have sent a list."

She winced in frustration. "Do you have any ideas about where to find a person on Bilioth?"

"There are over fifteen thousand persons on Bilioth. May I suggest a companion for tonight? We maintain a select list of expert comfort workers. Do you prefer male or female partners? Do you have a fetish in mind? Or any medical restrictions to be accommodated?"

"That will be all."

The Vel.2 didn't move.

"What?"

"May I offer you a refresher? Hydration is essential for optimum health."

"Duly noted." She reached up and took a drink from the Vel.2's outstretched tray. It scooted away.

"Wait!"

The machine sped back, resting at the edge of the pool, the tiny blue light the only indication it was listening.

"How did Sharm Karpolo die?"

"Sharm Karpolo fell to his death in Kikiki Valley, while attempting to jump from the back of one Jaisenet Bird to the back of another."

Vole gasped at the image. Was that why Arpina Karpolo was so bitter? But...if they had let her son fall to his death, why had the birds saved Vole?

"And the other AUD prize winners? Where are they? Are they alive?"

"According to my information, the four most recent champions will be gathering in Vortex Park for Solstice in five days' time."

"And you can't tell me if they're on-planet. Right?"

"That is correct."

"Could you tell me if they were off planet?"

"I'm afraid do not have that information."

"Okay. Send me a schedule of activities for Solstice. That will be all."

"Very good."

The Vel.2 zipped off.

Mist rose in ribbons toward the crimson sky, now faintly sprinkled with stars. The pool's surface ruffled pleasantly in the duskwind. Vole knew that she shouldn't stay in the heat for too long. But the guttural amphibian orchestra had started up their serenade again, their croaks all around her like gentle doors opening and closing. Her feet brushed the porcelain pool bottom, slick and hard, and she pushed herself back to floating. A voice in her head said, *fish don't even know there is such a thing as water.*

A satellite tracked overhead, a tiny orange firefly skimming the exosphere. Flight was overrated in the evolution of humankind. Manufacturing the H2O molecule was the more important innovation. Making water was what had allowed humans to colonize space, to bio-form potential planets, and save depleted ones.

Water was life.

Vole drifted, letting go of all thought. Her brain was making halting progress down a blind path, an exhausted animal moving stubbornly onward, toward a destination she couldn't see, but could only sense. A faint scent had replaced the flowers' sharp sweet, this one closer to the silky musk of human skin. But who's? Vole's eyes drifted closed. Her lips submerged with a faint taste of salt. What was she walking toward? Something comforting, something she needed. Vole inhaled.

Pain erupted in her nostrils. Suddenly awake, she emerged coughing and spitting, elated by a crystalline thought that had appeared in her mind. *That was it!* She let out an exuberant whoop. A couple on a far-off walkway turned their heads, then hurried on. *Water.* Wherever the pathogen had originated had to be a growth-rich environment, someplace where a virus could mutate easily and rapidly. *Someplace wet.*

Stepping into the cool night air, Vole grabbed a lodging robe, pulled it over her moist skin, and hurried to visual Xan.

Xan smiled, but the deep circles under his brown eyes and his black hair, matted on one side, told Vole that he had been sleeping in the clinic, if he'd been able to rest at all.

"You're going to get sick, too, if you're not careful."

He laughed, slightly hysterical, then grew mock-serious. "Are you...wet?"

"A little bit." She paused. A breeze flowed through her French doors, carrying scents of green water and fresh wood. "I need you to look something up for me."

Vole had asked the Vel.2 as soon as she got out of the pool, but it had stated each time she had asked, no matter how she asked, that there were *no swampy places on Bilioth outside of the Jaisenet Reserve. Those ponds, in Kikiki Valley, were scrupulously maintained, by Scientist Arpina Karpolo.*

"How sure are we that this bug originated on Bilioth? Could it have come from a totally different ecosystem?"

"Of course," Xan shrugged. "Just find Patient Zero, cure him, and let Naivos deal with closing down the source. You're needed here."

"I'm working on it," she sighed, thinking about how little she'd learned from the Vel.2, wishing there were an obvious lead in the information. "How hard can it be to find one famous ship commander in a dinky resort colony?"

Xan sighed. "Maybe you should tell folks why you're there. Naivos is crabby, but she'd probably overlook any infractions right now."

"She's in a worse mood than before?" Vole had felt the rage even through the Forum Representative's rigid posture. "If I shared Oliason's medical records, she'd have my license in a heartbeat. Plus, she wanted you to do this, not me."

"I know, but this is my clinic. And I'm not trying to upset you. But...unfortunately, one of the MedGens revealed to Her Highness that..." He held up a syringe of blood-red fluid. "...this is all we have left of Alpha strain polymer."

"You've already used all the Alpha?"

He nodded his head tiredly. "It gets worse. The virus has mutated."

"So, you're on to Beta strain?" She adjusted the robe. Its thick material suddenly felt clammy against her skin.

"You know Lafford. Tourists and soldiers, cargo haulers and stateless colonials. Everyone mingling freely."

Her skin tightened. "What strain are you up to, Xan?"

His voice went flat. "Foxtrot."

"Foxtrot? Are you kidding me?"

Silence crackled on the interface. Vole took a deep breath, imagining the whirring MedGens working night and day to spin up so much polymer. "We're going to need more machines."

"They're on order. But...Naivos is talking about a quarantine."

"She wants to close the portals? We'd have sixty thousand cases inside of a month. With a fifteen percent mortality rate...no. She must be bluffing."

"Or not." He shrugged. "If we can give her what she wants, all of this goes away. And you get a much-needed break."

The room slowed down, emerging more sharply. Vole's scalp tingled, something dawning on her. "Oh, Xan. You saw this coming. You sent me off-station to protect me from being trapped there."

He swallowed. "I know how you feel about being trapped."

They stared into each other's faces. A blip in the connection confirmed the three rimeters of space between them. Xan's attention moved to the door, out of frame.

He flattened his hair with a palm, his voice growing louder. "Ah, Madame Representative. My colleague and I were just talking about you."

A face appeared next to his. Quadrant Forum Representative Natova Naivos' silver hair and cunning expression seemed better suited to a broadcast studio than the bright clinic. She wore embroidered robes and sparkling jewelry. Her voice was deep, mellifluous, and ancient. The speech of an uncrowned queen, Vole thought, more than a politician.

"Medic Ublion. I trust you're enjoying your...rather expensive fieldtrip?"

Vole's face flushed annoyingly. "Madame Naivos."

"I heard about your visit to the Jaisenet Reserve. You are not authorized as my envoy."

Vole kept her voice professional. "I am aware. I merely asked for help. But I imagine you heard how eager Scientist Karpolo was to assist us with our outbreak."

Naivos' face didn't change. "Arpina has a job to do. And so do you."

"Of course." Wet hair tickled Vole's shoulders. "Speaking of respect for a protected species, you sent me to the Aviary Club. Are you personally aware of what happens there?"

"Of course." Naivos' gray eyes narrowed. "Very little takes place in this quadrant without my knowledge, Medic Ublion. I advise you to tread lightly on things that don't concern Lafford Waystation."

"What if the birds were the source of infection?"

"Arpina assures me they are not." The older woman's mouth twitched. "Let's focus. I assume you've spoken to Commander Olia-son. I'm sure he was glad to be given the polymer. What did he say about the source of his disease?"

"Unfortunately, Madame, no one on this planet seems to know where he is."

Naivos showed no surprise. "Whom have you asked, besides poor Arpina?"

Vole's cheeks burned with humiliation, which struck her as absurd. She didn't remember the last time someone had been able to make her feel that much emotion about anything.

"I must have misunderstood your instructions, Madame."

Naivos' hands rose in an exasperated gesture. "I said look for Olia-son at the Aviary, because he is a partial owner of that awful place. It had nothing to do with the birds, you linear-thinking lab rat. Hon-estly. If you can't find him, and lock down whatever infectious crag he fell into, I really may be forced to quarantine Waystation Lafford."

"That seems extreme," Vole sputtered. "And needlessly dangerous."

"Medic." Naivos slapped the desk. "If you had kept Oli on-station, we wouldn't be in this predicament."

"That's true," Vole said quietly. "I believed him when he said he'd come back in a few hours. It didn't occur to me that he'd be so craven as to run."

"Yes. You should have done your job. Regulations are clear on that point." Naivos' eyes moved to her taeki, reading a message or checking the time.

Xan shook his head, voice rising. "No, no. That's if a person has a *known infectious disease*. Oliason's was the first case of a brand-new virus. Vole had no way of knowing what it was."

"There's more to this story." Vole flipped the wet hair off her skin. "Why would you run from people who only want to help you?"

"Perhaps he doesn't trust medics," Naivos said tartly. "What is your next move, Medic Ublion? Tell me it's not to go disturb another protected species. If you commit a third infraction, I will be forced to recommend the med board rescind your license."

Hostile patients were either in more pain than they could handle, or they were hiding something. Vole smiled confidently. "That hovercab driver you sent to the space port."

"I sent no driver. I assumed you could navigate a tourist town on your own."

Xan made a baffled face. "Me neither."

"I was picked up by a young woman. We got in an accident. A pretty serious one. She was taken away by Emergency Services. She definitely knows Oliason. And a lot more, I suspect."

"Great." Naivos played absently with a silver chain at her neck. "I'll give you one more day, Medic Ublion. After that, Lafford goes on lockdown, and I'll recommend quarantine to the station forum. Until then, I'll be aboard my ship."

The platinum head disappeared. Vole sighed deeply, suddenly exhausted.

"Medic Ublion." Xan's dark eyes flashed. "What the hell is this about an accident?"

Chapter Seven

A Heated Exchange

After she'd calmed Xan down and urged him to sleep, Vole followed her own advice by putting on dry night clothes and going to bed. She had only a vague idea of what to do next, with her one remaining day on Bilioth. She didn't share her dark suspicion that Naivos would impose a quarantine and implement martial no matter what, for reasons of her own. Xan had enough on his mind.

After a minute of wondering why she liked the Good Ship's soft bed better than her bunk on Lafford, Vole realized it was because the only sounds were leaves shifting in the duskwind, and distant screams of laughter. She had always loved the Waystation's soft, mechanical heartbeat, the thrumming under the floors and in the walls. But now, as she closed her eyes and drifted to sleep, Vole didn't miss it.

It was after midnight when the lodging interface chimed. "Announcement: Guest, you have a visitor."

Vole pulled her pillow over her head. She'd been dreaming about suffocation again, limbs and torsos pressing into her, and a smell of metal. Under the chaos gleamed a thread of warmth, like a familiar hand, just out of reach.

"Announcement: Guest, you have a visitor."

She groaned. "I can't. I don't know anyone."

"It is a...*Mr. Nyppio*. This is your third and final announcement. Shall I request an alternate meeting time?"

Vole sat up, wide awake. "No, tell him to wait."

Pulling on her tunic and grabbing her bag, Vole hurried downstairs. People often found her to confess clandestine ailments. Vole had saved many lives in the dead of the night. The tall man stood fidgeting in the large door frame between the bright lobby and low-lit bar. His tunic and white braids seemed dustier than before, keen amber eyes bloodshot.

Vole motioned. "We can speak in the bar, if you're more comfortable."

"Sorry to disturb, Miss." Nyppio edged into the room, which was empty but for a bartender Vel.2, standing like a silver angel under the glow of lamplight, blue eye steady. "It took me a while to find you. Didn't peg you for a Good Ship kinda gal."

"No?" Vole offered a tight, professional smile, noting the *Miss*. "What kind of gal did you peg me as?"

She followed him to a booth near a bank of large windows overlooking the lodging's glass-and-metal wings. They joined the gleaming starship seamlessly, lining the dark gardens in a wide V, the pool shimmering beyond black trees.

"Not as a kept lady, no offense." He winked.

He wasn't there for medical advice. Vole sat on an upholstered bench, tossing her bag to one side. "You don't know. I might be."

"Fine." Nyppio gazed at her indulgently. "Let me buy you a drink, if your *arrangement* will allow."

The Vel.2 moved to take their order.

"I'll have a glass of...local wine," Vole said.

"Amber ale."

"What's going on, Mr. Nyppio?"

"Just Nyppio, please." He smiled, his weathered face crinkling beneath his white whiskers. "You're still seeking Bo Oliason."

"I am." Was it odd that Nyppio framed it as a fact, not a question?

"I heard about what happened."

"You mean me getting thrown out of the Aviary?"

He sighed. "Yelling and carrying on about leaving a message for Oli."

"I need to find him, urgently. Beyond urgently."

The Vel.2 rolled over with their drinks. Nyppio raised his glass to her. "Good health."

"I could really use your help." She caught his eye. "It's a matter of life and death."

"I see." His smile disappeared. "I've been around a long while. People who care about the success of this place like to talk to me."

"And these people say what, exactly?"

"There's concern about anything that might interfere with Bilioth's continued popularity. Locals want visitors to be happy, to feel free to do whatever they're not allowed to do in the rest of the diaspora. You've seen the art, the architecture, the way people express themselves."

With heroic effort, Vole kept her eyes from rolling. "Sure."

"I got to thinking about our meeting."

"Our chance encounter, in a restaurant that just happens to be across the street from Oliason's place of business? That you, apparently, keep an eye on."

He made a show of sipping ale. "Oli sold his stake in The Aviary some weeks ago. No one's seen him since."

Vole thought about Naivos' threats. Minna didn't know where Oliason was, she'd said so in the hovercab. Vole saw no other option but to tell the truth and risk the consequences. "I saw Commander Oliason seven days ago. I'm a Command Medic from Lafford. Thousands of lives depend on my finding him."

Nyppio's face didn't move. "A Command Medic, working to save thousands of lives? That sounds like an excellent job. You must be anxious to get back to it."

"If you think you're helping Oliason by covering up his whereabouts, I can tell you that nothing is further from the truth." She glared at him.

"I'm trying to help you."

"I'm waiting for you to say one true thing." Vole crossed her arms. "Ale's not your drink. And Oliason is on-planet. If he weren't, you wouldn't show up here at this hour to throw me off the trail. The question is, what are the people sent you so afraid I'll find?"

His eye flicked toward the lobby door. "What's my real drink?"

Vole tipped her head to one side. "Whiskey. Rye if you can find it. Corn mash if you can't."

His amber eyes widened. "You're kinda scary."

"I'm going back to bed. Thanks for the drink." She pushed away the goblet, untouched.

"Wait!" Nyppio motioned for her to stay put. "I'll share what little I know, if you'll just...let me say it in my own way. It'll take a few minutes."

Vole settled back into the booth. "We've got all night."

"Oli has a cargo fleet of twelve ships, piloted by all manner of scallywags and adventurers. Most of them are people he met crewing for his AUD team."

"*Pirates*, I think is the technical term. Go on."

"They aren't thieves. Just a bunch of thrill seekers, looking for fun and opportunity."

"And I bet Oliason is happy to oblige. For a fee." She swirled the garnet wine. "Which places him...?"

He made a helpless gesture. "Oli is known for paying everyone their wages, generously, and on time. Right now, his people are hurting. He owes everyone something. Money, favors, a chance to compete. More and more of them are arriving for Solstice now, with stuff he told them to deliver, and guests he invited."

"I told you," Vole said, putting her pinkie in the glass and tasting the wine. It was pungent, and alive. "He's not well. I'm not surprised he doesn't want to see people right now."

"Understood. But these people are highly motivated, and they're adventurers. Nothing gets in their way. They've scoured every inch of Bilioth. Oli doesn't want to be found."

Four men entered the lobby, out of Vole's sightlines. They argued loudly and drunkenly about a go-cart race.

"It was so cheating. That guy always cheats."

"Not this time, dumbass."

"Yeah. You're allowed to sharpen the hubcaps."

"Nuh uh, the rules besifically...sebifically...spefically..."

Nyppio's eyes moved uneasily from the doorway, back to her.

"Good morning, gentlemen. May we assist you?" offered the reception Vel.2.

There were three loud crashes. Vole sighed. Nyppio stared fixedly at a bubble in his glass.

"May I assist you?" The Vel.2 repeated.

"Sure, you can," said the deepest of the voices.

Metal tore, and the lobby came to life, alarms pinging, the interface calmly instructing guests to shelter in place. Vole's fingers twitched involuntarily over the place where her pistol ought to have been. She stood and slung the bag over her shoulder.

Nyppio reached out a hand uselessly as she sprang to the lobby. A pile of smoking metallic limbs shorted out in a hail of sparks. Four fit-looking men dressed in typical Bilioth tunics strode down the north wing, their backs to her. They moved with silent intent, like soldiers or criminals. The tallest of the men held a Vel.2's severed mechanical arm; the one that had unlocked Vole's door when she'd arrived, with its universal key-lase.

She walked back into the bar.

"Were they planning to hurt me, or just scare me a little?"

"Arson, is all. For now." Nyppio spoke softly. He drained his glass and walked out the lobby doors.

Vole moved to the windows, just stepping through the doors as water rained down from sprinklers on the ceiling, hitting her scalp with cold droplets. Her wing had begun winking prettily, golden flames against black velvet. Distant sirens whooped. People had begun emerging on paths and balconies to watch the fire, their eyes glowing like nocturnal predators.

Chapter Eight

What an Interesting Case

At dawn, Vole was pedaling a kolmi across a ring road to a huge, green park where the eight Playplex districts converged. Early morning joggers smiled and saluted her in passing, as if she, too, were here for her health.

By the time Vole reached Vortex Park Medotel, she was sweating. On a street of ostentatious theme lodgings and restaurants, the building itself was blessedly generic.

She checked her taeki one last time, realizing as she did that Naivos never intended to supply a records waiver. Vole didn't understand the game she'd been sent to take part in, but it was becoming clearer that she was being used. Somehow, that notion spurred her on, setting her will into a blade of stubborn will. If scientists hadn't risked moving forward without enough data, humans would never have left Earth. Vole was going to find the source of Sairasma, if she had to shred her license and set it aflame herself.

She entered the Medotel. It was gleamingly empty, staffed by Vel.2 MedGens with expensive-looking, transformable frames. The machines looked like they could do ten tasks at once. A thread of jealousy snagged in Vole's chest.

"Good morning. How can we help?" the closest MedGen said pleasantly.

Vole smiled uselessly. "I'm Minna Tegg's Medic."

The MedGen flashed a beam across Vole's eyes. She braced herself. Would the machine throw her out, or merely ask her to leave?

"Very Good, Medic Ublion. I have sent her chart to your taeki," the Vel.2 replied.

"You sent me an electronic chart?" Vole stammered. Naivos must have produced the waiver after all.

"Yes. The data is non-transferable and will erase if taken off-surface."

"What a great innovation. Is this way of doing things specific to Vortex Park?"

"My information is yes. At Vortex Park, we take pride in efficiency."

So, nothing to do with Naivos. Vole thought for a moment. "Can I have other charts? I'm also Bo Oliason's medic."

"I have sent his information to your taeki. May I further assist you?"

She checked her device. Oliason had last visited the Medotel three years before, for a sprain suffered in a climbing accident. Nothing else in his chart caught her notice, except that he had weighed roughly a third more at that visit than she'd seen him on-station. The contact information was unchanged. She sent another message, though she assumed Oliason would ignore it.

The MedGen stood at attention. It reminded her of her machines during the war, more dependable than human staff.

"Take me to Minna Tegg. But first, I need the restroom."

The MedGen ushered Vole down a wide hallway, past some intriguing labs and empty treatment rooms.

"Down the hallway, on the left side. I will wait for you here." The machine positioned itself with its crawler tracks against a wall.

Vole found herself alone in a wide hallway stocked with supplies. She opened every drawer she could find, but despite the Medotel's opulence, the items within were standard canisters, tubes, and sterile packages. Vole irradiated her hands, then stole as much as her bag would hold.

"Thanks," she said to her guide. "I feel better now."

The MedGen's tracks squeaked softly as they proceeded. Vole wondered how much deference the gleaming white machine would show her. If she ordered it to follow all the way to the spaceport, could she find a way to get it on board the shuttle?

Minna lay hooked to an IV, asleep in a pool of spit. Devoid of jewelry, she looked smaller, her mohawk reduced to a maroon nest. Vole studied her chart thoughtfully. The girl had been on-planet for just over a year. Her occupation was listed as *dancer*. She had reported for standard care twice, with a third visit when one of her piercings had become infected. The only interesting item was her admission after the accident. In addition to a *broken femur, torn ligaments,* and *a concussion,* Minna presented an *acute skin condition that did not respond to normal protocols.*

She had Sairasma.

The chart had indicated Minna was heavily sedated. But sometimes even drugged patients could be shaken awake. Vole moved closer, bending over the sleeping girl, hands reaching toward her shoulders.

"May I help you?" A tall man in clean white scrubs entered, his surgically perfected face and blinding teeth almost too beautiful to look at.

"Oh," Vole stepped back awkwardly. "Hello."

"I'm Grigg Vidsonnen, attending."

Vole hastily introduced herself, making sure to include Quadrant Rep Naivos' name.

"Ah, I see," Vidsonnen nodded gravely. "How may we help?"

"I was concerned after Minna...your patient...and I were in the accident. I was very fortunate to escape with only a few contusions. But she was...I couldn't come before now."

"Did you suffer a concussion too? Vidsonnen gave her an appraising look. "You look a bit...forgive me...disheveled. I'd be happy to examine you."

"I'm fine." She waved him off. "Thank you."

"If you're sure." Vidsonnen looked toward the door.

Two Vel.2s appeared, moving to attention on either side of the opening. Security. Vole was faintly surprised it had taken them so long to arrive.

"Medic Vidsonnen, I'm still a bit worried about Miss Tegg."

"I assure you," he said, his blue eyes growing steely. "She's getting the best of care."

"Oh, I know," Vole said, overloud. "I'm so glad she's here. Since I...know how distressed she was about...her rash."

His face didn't move, though his eyes went to Minna's blanket-draped form.

"Well. Glad we could put your mind at ease. Please, relax and enjoy your vacation here on Bilioth."

Vole scrolled through Minna's chart desperately. "Uhm. Just...while I have you."

"You...had a medical question?" He tipped his head to one side, eyes gleaming with interest.

"Yes! Yes." Vole smiled. "This technique of cold surgery on the ligaments. I've never observed it in practice. But, such a clever idea, knocking back inflammation before it begins."

Vidsonnen tented his fingers, studying her. "Thank you. I wish I could invite you to observe, but there are no acute cases at the moment. Because we have so much trauma here, in the Playplex, we've developed some techniques..."

He launched into a list of tweaks to standard procedure. Vole was torn between being impressed by the facility's inventiveness, and amazed that they had time for such minor details. He finished speaking, looking at her expectantly.

"It must be great to have the resources to...perfect...best practices." She stopped herself before the words *play with* popped out, hastily adding. "What are the most common kinds of trauma you see?"

His arms fell to his sides. "Oh, the stories I could share with you. If we had time, Medic Ublion. I don't often get a chance to confer with off-planet colleagues."

"Please. Our clinic is but a humble Waystation, no bells or whistles."

"Don't be modest. Lafford is a large, strategically important base. And your practice must be fascinating. You see real folks, with health concerns they didn't deliberately bring upon themselves." He sighed deeply. "My patients go out of their way to imperil themselves, for no other reason than because it makes them feel *alive*."

They laughed. His chuckle was high and absurd, contrasting sharply with his perfectly-sculpted face.

"Ah, people. The bane of any Medic's existence, am I right?"

He patted her arm absently. "I sense you and I are very alike."

She moved a step away. "Oh?"

In her dusty tunic, hair smelling like smoke, face no doubt still sheened with sweat, Vole felt like a separate species from Vidsonnen's clean perfection.

"Oh yes. People like us, we're obsessed. Using an unfortunate hovercab accident as an excuse to sneak into a provincial clinic and learn anything you can?"

"I'm sorry," Vole stammered. "Did it seem like I was poaching your advances?"

He giggled. "There's no use denying it. I see through you."

"You...do?"

He opened his arms in a welcoming gesture. "Of course. You didn't come here to steal ideas. You came because you can't do anything else. Healing the sick is so much more compelling than any resort vacation. Am I right? Why go up in a blimp, when you can improve protocols for preserving necrotic tissue?"

"Medic Vidsonnen," Vole smiled up at him, genuinely charmed. "You're a very perceptive man."

Two hours later, after a detailed tour of the facility that left Vole aching with envy, the two medics sat in a pristine caf. A tray of pastries sat between them, each item missing a surgically precise sample, with a damning trail of crumbs leading to Vidsonnen's plate.

"You really should try the lemon square," he said, motioning.

Though she was more than full, Vole swallowed a minute taste of the tart yellow cake, wishing she were still hungry enough to eat more. But lunch was over. Soon, her host would insist on going back to work, and she still had no leads for finding Oliason.

"I was wondering...other than the cold surgery, which I gather is standard here, was Minna Tegg's case unusual?"

"You're not her medic?"

"Not really. I came here to ask her a question. I only rode in the cab with Minna and provided emergency care. I didn't examine her. I didn't know she had a venereal rash until I looked at her chart."

There was a long pause while Vidsonnen pierced her with his gaze. "In these times of data restriction, one doesn't know whom to trust. But I will extend my faith in you, Vole, if only to reward you for letting me prattle on. Minna's rash is unlike anything I've seen. It's causing her such intense discomfort, she can't keep herself from scratching to the point where..."

Vole sighed. "She's harming herself. Her lymph nodes are swollen and blue. And she is beginning to have trouble breathing."

"Ah, it comes clear. You've decided to trust me, too." He sat back. "You have an outbreak on Lafford."

"They're threatening to declare a state of emergency."

"Martial law?"

"Grigg." Vole chose her words carefully. "I believe Commander Bo Oliason knows the location of the hot spot."

Vidsonnen tisked disapprovingly. "Bo Oliason."

"Or as I call him, Patient Zero."

Vidsonnen listened raptly while she explained.

"Very well handled. But. you spun up a polymer on your own, rather than requisition Central?"

"No time," Vole said. "This thing has been coming fast and furious. Mutating like mad."

"So, you just created a polymer, without a study or any help from above." He made a clapping motion. "Bravo, Medic. Cure the beast, before it spreads."

"We can knock it back in most cases, but not all. And we have no information about recurrence."

"Oh yes. Colonies and shiploads of people, infecting one another with every interaction." He grimaced. "What about immunization?"

"Quite possible." She blew out breath. "But do you know how long it would take?"

"Years."

"And delivery is chaotic. So many people off the grid, rejecting traditional medicine. Look around you. You think the weirdos on this planet would respond to a Command summons to come get shot with a new substance?"

He smiled kindly. "I see your point. Many folks would rather risk death than trust the government."

She sighed. "The same government that saved them from the Vel.1s."

"Nothing will stop this if you don't seal the source."

"And the only one who knows where it is has evaporated."

They sat in silence.

"I'm glad you're sympathetic to my quest here. Because I was considering stealing several of your MedGens. I need them more than you do."

"Not if we find Oli." He leaned toward her, so close she could smell his spicy cologne. "Do you have polymer for my patient? You said you were concerned about her."

"Unfortunately, I have only one dose." Vole's hand involuntarily covered her bag. "I'd be serving Oliason a death sentence if I give it to Minna."

Vidsonnen's brows furrowed ever so slightly. "I have a proposal for you. If we don't find Oliason by the time you are due for the shuttle tonight..."

"We cure Minna. And I get two, no three MedGens to bring back to Lafford with me."

"Done."

After a split second of hesitation, Vole shook Vidsonnen's out-stretched hand.

Chapter Nine

Disguises

An hour later, Vidsonnen and Vole were speeding across the desert in his luxurious, shiny black Leona. It was the most beautiful vehicle Vole had ever seen, with a hover so smooth she barely felt them moving. She was beginning to respect Vidsonnen's unabashed enthusiasm for excellence. With a tiny flick of his hand, her companion raised the bubble, closing out the dust clouds that blew in from the north, and started up low strains of instrumental music.

"Thank you again. Though, I could get to the Reserve on my own, you know. I walked there, last time."

"Not a particularly safe thing to do," His eyes behind sunglasses flashed a disapproving sidelong glance. "Did you do no research? The plain is infested by poisonous insects and toxic bloom."

"No time to prepare." She smiled. "I did start to feel a little loopy."

"I'm glad to come. I've always wanted to see the Jaisenet Refuge. Arpina will never grant me a permit."

"You know Scientist Karpolo?"

"Arpy the Harpy? Yes, we've met, and I've tried to engage her in conversation about scientific matters. But she never entertains, except for the occasional sad dinner with her son's friends. She refuses all invitations. My parties are legendary. Only a misanthrope would pass them up."

Without his lab coat, Vidsonnen wore a clean white shirt, and slacks that managed to be tailored and outdoorsy at the same time. In his dark glasses and gleaming black hair, the large man was so absurdly debonair, Vole felt like the drab rodent she'd named herself after.

"This is a small planet, isn't it?"

"Oh, yes. Permanent residents are well acquainted with one another's business. As a medic I keep my mouth shut, of course. But I can tell you, as a colleague, that I knew poor Sharm Karpolo. He came into the Medotel far too often. I wasn't the only one who worried that being raised on the Preserve wasn't good for the boy. Watching his mother anthropomorphize them made him think those birds were his friends."

"Wait, is that your interest in the place?" Vole turned. "You think they murdered your patient?"

Vidsonnen's smile dropped away. "No. If anything, Sharm's death was a suicide." He waved his large hand. "We lose people every year. Bilioth is a dangerous planet to begin with, and people come here specifically to do crazy things. Sometimes it kills them."

"And people keep telling me to enjoy my time here, that it's so liberating. "

"The danger is nothing personal on the part of Bilioth herself. She's just a simple planet. It's not her fault she's been turned into an adventure park."

"Someone told me the locals don't want Oliason found, because it might give the adventure park a bad reputation."

"Really?" He gave her a sharp look. "Well. It shouldn't surprise us if there are interested parties who don't mind an epidemic running rampant off-surface, as long as no one connects it to Bilioth."

"Who might these parties be, specifically?"

He shrugged. "I could guess, but there are too many possibilities."

The scene passing outside the bubble was ochre ground met in equal measure by rose-violet sky. Vole didn't recognize their path, but a splash of mustard-yellow in the far distance must be the fields of flowers she'd crossed. *If only she'd sampled them.*

"Grigg?" They'd moved to first names during lunch. "Guess anyway?"

"We have two kinds of people. The adventurers, who fly Zeppelins over lava beds, consort with merwhales, that sort of thing. The most famous of these are the Daredevils, because of the prize, but they are by no means the only idiots who pull crazy stunts. And then, there are the opportunists, who rarely leave the Playplex. You see them pretending to be tourists, or party guests, when in reality they own all the entertainments, or at least, they run them for offshore partnerships. These are the more dangerous players."

"Because of money." A bug splatted on the bubble, leaving a black, oozing carcass. Before it could slide into Vole's view, a robotic arm moved to squeegee the mess away. The music shifted to a stringed, soothing melody.

"Of which there is plenty. They provide whatever the adventurers need, or want, or think they might want. The latest, trendiest thrill. Which can be any activity that offers that rare, life-altering rush no one else has experienced."

"Including the exploitation of sentient creatures." Vole shook her head, brow furrowing. From a great distance, she observed herself feeling intense, boiling rage. She breathed slowly, fingering the meds in her bag. "I can't believe we fought a war, so people could waste their lives on this nonsense."

Vidsonnen snapped off the music. He slowed the Leona over a series of deep gashes in rock, layered in ochre, sienna and gold. "What do you see?"

Vole crossed her arms. The shimmering desert below mirrored high, white clouds in a deep rose sky. The horizon was a line of graphite atop wine-brown desert. The chasms below them opened to forested waterfalls, leading to vast canyons hanging with dead-branched, black shrubs that looked vaguely like spiders. Vole sensed that if she were to climb out of the byl, she'd find ten different animals that could kill her, and of those, half would actively want to.

"I see wilderness. Wild, beautiful, and hostile."

"Exactly. That is what the founders of the Playplex saw, too. They were idealists. They wanted Bilioth's human colony to be a place for mind expansion, for re-invention. A path to enlightenment, if you will, by way of facing fears."

She snorted. "So this is what Utopia looks like?"

Vidsonnen gazed at her piercingly over the tops of his glasses. "It was, in the beginning. Truly. The Playplex itself was only permitted for a standard year. The thought was to learn what we could, then let Bilioth go back to nature. But the Authority has allowed tourists to keep coming for fifteen years." He started the byl again with a faint whirr.

They rode in silence for a few minutes. Then Vole said, face flushing, "Am I the only person who thinks it's wrong to be off adventuring so soon after our species was almost wiped out?"

He maneuvered the byl over maroon vegetation that looked like a carpet of living brains. "I think you're being a bit unfair, Medic. Most of the people here are either too young to have served, or they're like you."

"What do you mean, *like me*?" Vole felt the sting of being transparent to anyone who looked. She missed Xan's understanding that while they spent all their time together, she couldn't give him the touch he yearned for. She was safe on Lafford. Xan had made sure of it. Her stomach tingled with unease. She wanted to turn the Leona around and head straight back to the space port.

Vidsonnen steered them across another wide breach in the ground. "My dear Medic Ublion. You're enviable. You actually served the human race. Doing something real."

She almost choked. "Real? Are you joking?"

"Not at all." He gazed at her through mirrored glass. "Please don't be offended. Can you keep a secret? Never mind, I know you can't. I was in the war too, on Battle Station Stanwyn."

The skin around Vole's eyes stung slightly as Vidsonnen's words sunk in.

"At Xunza?" It had been one of the fiercest battles of the war.

"Yes." He gritted his teeth. "I stayed on station, but it was grim."

Vole studied his face, seeing it differently. "Stanwyn Station was destroyed by fire."

He stared at his knuckles on the steering console.

"You were burned," Vole said softly.

Vidsonnen said tightly, "I was wearing gloves, mercifully, so my surgical career could continue, after some work. We did a wonderful job on my face, don't you think?"

"Yes." She touched his sleeve, catching his eye. "Your disguise is very convincing."

He made a wry expression, "I have had twelve major surgeries and as many procedures. Naturally, the money had to come from somewhere."

"So you came to Bilioth?"

He nodded, his cheeks dimpling into a half-smile. "You're a smart one. I could tell the moment I saw you trolling for data at the front desk."

Vole sat back. "You gave them permission to share the files with me."

"I knew there was a Command Medic on planet, because you used the code when you called the MedGens for Minna. I was curious."

The landscape was shifting to the bisque color that signaled the start of the Reserve. "In that case, you should just drop me. It might be dangerous to be seen together."

His laugh sounded richly amused. "Are you kidding? I'm having far too much fun. This is an adventure. If I want to feel safe, Medic Ublion, I'll visit space."

She couldn't help smiling at that.

Chapter 10, Disguises

Vole and Vidsonnen walked side by side into the Reserve, sweating through their clothes, faces flushed in the midday sun. Vidsonnen pointed out poisonous plants and insects, sharing stories of the patients he'd seen who'd been stung, mauled, or sent on hallucinatory trips.

"They love to brag about it afterward. If they survive," he said cheerfully. "I'm very excited to be here, by the way. I'll take some images, so in case anyone asks I can say this visit is for the good of science. But now that we're here, what gives you the idea that the birds will help you? Didn't you ask them once already?"

"Karpolo chased me way before they could answer." Vole kicked a large stick out of her path. It promptly grew legs and skittered away.

"I'm out of options. The only other thing I can think of doing is to break into the spaceport and look for Oliason's ship."

"The Rausku is off planet." He wiped at his forehead with one hand.

"How do you know that?"

"I have everyone's contact information." He looked around protectively. "And I know everyone's secrets. Oli hasn't been to any healers, temples, or nightclubs for ages. It's not easy to hide here, outside the Playplex, and he's simply not been seen inside. Some people think he's dead. I did learn one thing, though."

"Did you come all the way out here just to humor me?" She pushed damp hair behind an ear. Her ankles were beginning to itch.

"I came for my patient. But also, curiosity. We people of science are nothing without wanting to find the answers, are we?"

"Granted, but it's not in your interest to help me find him."

"Oh, it is in a way. Then he gets saved, and I get to see the birds."

Vole almost stopped dead. Vidsonnen had never been to the Aviary. This knowledge made her like him even more. "What's the one thing, then? That you learned?"

He turned, waiting for her to catch up. "Someone, not Oli, ordered the Rausku into Hevoxin airspace some weeks ago, though exactly when is vague. What is sure is that whoever issued the instruction must be quite powerful. Oli's people wouldn't leave without him. Not unless they were coerced."

"Or if he ordered them to, correct?"

Vidsonnen paused. "I suppose. Look, are you sure the man you're chasing is really Bo Oliason?"

"Yes. Retina match. DNA match. He doesn't have a twin or a clone. Do you think his crew might be away to give the appearance that he's off on a cargo run? Give him time to recover?" She didn't add that without the polymer, he wasn't likely to.

"Do you know where he was before checking in to your clinic?"

"No. I was able to find out that he came in from an interplanetary transport."

"Public transpo?" Vidsonnen sounded horrified.

"I know," Vole said darkly. They reached the narrow passageway Vole had followed Karr'a'a'a'a through. "Over here."

The cool shade smelled of dirt and something that reminded Vole of rust. Vidsonnen fell in behind her as they filed down the path, onto the broad plateau with its circle of high, loaf-like rock formations.

"Amazing," Vidsonnen whispered.

Across the plane, a fiery crimson orb stood on one long, maroon foot, preening itself absently. One yellow eye fixed on them as they approached, then a whole Jaisenet head emerged, nostrils flaring.

Vole stepped forward and made an awkward bow.

"What are you doing?" Vidsonnen said in a soft, embarrassed voice.

The red bird cooed at him scoldingly, waving its wine-dark beak.

Vidsonnen's brows shot up. He bowed and muttered, "My apologies. Koo koo...kachoo."

Vole kicked him in the shin playfully and stepped past. "Keoka'a? I am Vole."

The fiery creature bent its neck in a gracious posture and cawed out a version of Vole's name.

"Oh my god," Vidsonnen smiled. "It said Vole."

"Now you."

Vidsonnen introduced himself, gesticulating grandly. "At your service."

Keoka'a cooed Vidsonnen's name. head rising to full height, brandishing a bronze crest like a lacey crown so they had to squint into the sun to keep looking.

"Magnificent. And knows it."

"May we speak with you?" Vole asked. The bird seemed to laugh. It shook its head from side to side.

"Yes?"

Shadows flicked across the landscape, birds high above, others seeming to circle nearby. Vole kept eye contact with the bird's golden eyes.

"Keoka'a. May I call you *friend*?"

Keoka'a sang Vole's name in its bird voice and inclined its head in what appeared to be agreement. Vidsonnen crossed his arms, muttering.

Vole made hand gestures to illustrate her words, ignoring Vidsonnen's amused look. "Does your migration...where your flock travels...take you anyplace very wet? Swampy? With standing water, maybe?"

The bird regarded her visitors for a moment, then with seeming effort, said, "Nah."

"Thank you," Vole continued, "Can you tell me...do other animals live in moisture? Wet place? In the wilds of the planet, perhaps? Far from the desert here?"

The bird's golden eyes fluttered. "Yek."

Vole nodded. "Yek? Yes? Is there any way to tell me where? I have asked the humans, and they say no such place exists."

"Vole," Vidsonnen said from behind her.

Keoka'a screeched alarmingly, throwing her head back and filling the valley with noise. She stood and stretched her wings.

"Medic Ublion," he repeated more urgently.

Vole kept eye contact with Keoka'a. "I'm sorry. It's just..."

Keoka'a flew away in a rush of red wings, screeching angrily.

"Wait!" Vole felt a hand grab her elbow and steer her into shadows. Vidsonnen's voice lost all urbane softness. "Airships, one o'clock, Medic. Take cover."

Vidsonnen pulled Vole into a narrow crevasse between halves of a cracked granite loaf. Gravel dusted her head and shoulders, making her sputter. Her mouth tasted like mud. Her scalp stung where a falling stone pinged it on the way down. Adrenaline surged through Vole, as familiar as the fear that creeping up her back. She willed it away, her senses turning sharp.

Outside, the bright valley filling with moving shadows, swooping and screaming with rage. Behind that came the sound of propellers, and then a booming. Rockets.

"Why are we hiding?" she panted. "Whoever it is wouldn't shoot people, would they?"

"They would if they didn't want witnesses." He tried to wipe his glasses clean. "You don't want them to see you, either. Third strike, you lose your license to practice medicine, isn't that what you told me?"

She rubbed her face, hands gritty. Vidsonnen stood in an alert stance, sweat running down his now dull hair, white shirt ruined. He smiled, looking like a different man.

"What are they doing? They can't be using rockets to hunt."

He craned his neck to peer outside. "I suspect they're giving looky-loos a special view of the birds. You know, *if you thought the Aviary was cool, how about disturbing a whole nesting ground?* That kind of thing is big business here."

The valley echoed with the sound of a hundred or more Jaisenets, screeching and howling angrily. A rocket whizzed and exploded, followed by a second. The ground under their feet began to rumble, gravel falling, ricocheting off the sides of the narrow space. Bullets hit stone, a dozen short pops.

The stone hallway began to rock and pitch, rocks cascading down and hitting Vole in the face. She barely avoided a long shard slicing vertically like a knife. Her elbow jarred painfully as she jumped away, eyes blinking away sand. "This isn't worth it. Let's get out of here."

"Be careful." His voice was pinched. "They don't know what they're doing. They're just...stupid opportunists...ripping off tourists."

Vidsonnen lurched forward, leaning on the wall. A narrow band of light hit a red stain blossoming across his back.

"Grigg. You've been hit."

"I noticed that too," he panted.

Vole grabbed coagulant foam from her bag and found a wide gash in the back of his head. She sprayed. "Where else are you hurt?"

"Just a few pieces of shrapnel, nothing serious," he rasped. His shirt was torn and bloody. Vole lifted it, spraying as she went. He sagged against his right shoulder, moving to sit on the ground.

"Medic Vidsonnen." She spoke loudly. "There are puncture wounds in your back. Is your lung collapsing?"

His voice was a ragged whisper. "Take the byl and run, Vole. Use your Command code. It will obey."

"Not without you." Her taeki was off grid. Vole cursed. "Stay with me. I'll flag down one of those airships. We'll get you to the Medotel."

She ripped open his shirt, revealing two large, ugly wounds, covered in white foam and blood. "I'm going to step out and get us a ride."

"Wait a second." He clutched at her tunic. "I need to tell you something."

"Make it quick." Vole tried to pry his fingers off, glad to see he had enough strength to hold her there.

"Minna was delirious when she was admitted."

"Let's elevate your feet, shall we?" Vole eased him to his side. She pressed on his wounds, making him gasp. "Tell me about Minna."

"She was in a semi-lucid state, and she kept muttering about *zoons. Magic mountain zoons.* She said, *Oli needs to protect their magic.* Or...something like that. It's not un...uncommon among our patients to speak of...magic."

Engines purred, further away. The airships were passing. Vole tried to pry her hem out of his clutches. "Zoons, Grigg? Minna talked about giant sentient worms? Ten Black Wizards from the children's book? With their magic well? You must have had a tough time keeping a straight face."

Vidsonnen's heart rate was dropping. The propellers grew fainter as they hovered away, leaving the valley quiet. But Vole had another idea. Karpolo.

"There could be magic Zoons anywhere in the universe, really," he rasped, "If they had a friend with a cargo ship."

"Grigg, this may hurt." Vole pushed into his back more forcefully. He grunted with pain.

"It's no use, darlin'," he whispered, his mouth opening to draw in air. "You're a good girl, you know. Special. You can't see it. But you are."

Vole wiped hair out of his face with a bloody hand. "Talk to me. What other cases are you working on?"

"Cure Minna. She's just a crazy little thing, she's got her whole life..." He coughed, then relaxed against the rock wall.

"Grigg," Vole ordered. "Come back to me."

Shale pressed painfully into Vole's knees as she tried to resuscitate him, first with her mini fib, then with her hands. From that angle, the symmetry of his reconstructed features made him look like something not-quite-human, nothing like her friend. Vole pushed away his now-limp hands, wondering what he had looked before the ship fire, what he had been like as a boy. He lay barely breathing, in a dark corridor of stone, his white shirt sticky with drying blood. Her eyes stung with the sadness and waste of it.

She hadn't felt that particular rage in years. It tasted like hot metal in her mouth, like chemicals and death.

Grigg Vidsonnen drew a final, rattling breath, and his long, slim body went still. Vole closed his eyes, whispering the words of blessing, then sat back. She drew a shaky breath, expecting panic, or battlefield numbness, to begin its work of tearing apart her psyche. But nothing happened. All Vole felt was calm, focused fury.

Her eye caught motion, a flash of silver and black. Vole stood, wiped her hands on her shirt, and walked into the valley.

Chapter Ten

Airships

Vole and Vidsonnen walked side by side into the Reserve, sweating through their clothes, faces flushed in the midday sun. Vidsonnen pointed out poisonous plants and insects, sharing stories of the patients he'd seen who'd been stung, mauled, or sent on hallucinatory trips.

"They love to brag about it afterward. If they survive," he said cheerfully. "I'm very excited to be here, by the way. I'll take some images, so in case anyone asks I can say this visit is for the good of science. But now that we're here, what gives you the idea that the birds will help you? Didn't you ask them once already?"

"Karpolo chased me way before they could answer." Vole kicked a large stick out of her path. It promptly grew legs and skittered away. "I'm out of options. The only other thing I can think of doing is to break into the spaceport and look for Oliason's ship."

"The Rausku is off planet." He wiped at his forehead with one hand.

"How do you know that?"

"I have everyone's contact information." He looked around protectively. "And I know everyone's secrets. Oli hasn't been to any healers, temples, or nightclubs for ages. It's not easy to hide here, outside the Playplex, and he's simply not been seen inside. Some people think he's dead. I did learn one thing, though."

"Did you come all the way out here just to humor me?" She pushed damp hair behind an ear. Her ankles were beginning to itch.

"I came for my patient. But also, curiosity. We people of science are nothing without wanting to find the answers, are we?"

"Granted, but it's not in your interest to help me find him."

"Oh, it is in a way. Then he gets saved, and I get to see the birds."

Vole almost stopped dead. Vidsonnen had never been to the Aviary. This knowledge made her like him even more. "What's the one thing, then? That you learned?"

He turned, waiting for her to catch up. "Someone, not Oli, ordered the Rausku into Hevoxin airspace some weeks ago, though exactly when is vague. What is sure is that whoever issued the instruction must be quite powerful. Oli's people wouldn't leave without him. Not unless they were coerced."

"Or if he ordered them to, correct?"

Vidsonnen paused. "I suppose. Look, are you sure the man you're chasing is really Bo Oliason?"

"Yes. Retina match. DNA match. He doesn't have a twin or a clone. Do you think his crew might be away to give the appearance that he's off on a cargo run? Give him time to recover?" She didn't add that without the polymer, he wasn't likely to.

"Do you know where he was before checking in to your clinic?"

"No. I was able to find out that he came in from an interplanetary transport."

"Public transpo?" Vidsonnen sounded horrified.

"I know," Vole said darkly. They reached the narrow passageway Vole had followed Karr'a'a'a'a through. "Over here."

The cool shade smelled of dirt and something that reminded Vole of rust. Vidsonnen fell in behind her as they filed down the path, onto the broad plateau with its circle of high, loaf-like rock formations.

"Amazing," Vidsonnen whispered.

Across the plane, a fiery crimson orb stood on one long, maroon foot, preening itself absently. One yellow eye fixed on them as they approached, then a whole Jaisenet head emerged, nostrils flaring.

Vole stepped forward and made an awkward bow.

"What are you doing?" Vidsonnen said in a soft, embarrassed voice.

The red bird cooed at him scoldingly, waving its wine-dark beak.

Vidsonnen's brows shot up. He bowed and muttered, "My apologies. Koo koo...kachoo."

Vole kicked him in the shin playfully and stepped past. "Keoka'a? I am Vole."

The fiery creature bent its neck in a gracious posture and cawed out a version of Vole's name.

"Oh my god," Vidsonnen smiled. "It said Vole."

"Now you."

Vidsonnen introduced himself, gesticulating grandly. "At your service."

Keoka'a cooed Vidsonnen's name. head rising to full height, brandishing a bronze crest like a lacey crown so they had to squint into the sun to keep looking.

"Magnificent. And knows it."

"May we speak with you?" Vole asked. The bird seemed to laugh. It shook its head from side to side.

"Yes?"

Shadows flicked across the landscape, birds high above, others seeming to circle nearby. Vole kept eye contact with the bird's golden eyes.

"Keoka'a. May I call you *friend*?"

Keoka'a sang Vole's name in its bird voice and inclined its head in what appeared to be agreement. Vidsonnen crossed his arms, muttering.

Vole made hand gestures to illustrate her words, ignoring Vidsonnen's amused look. "Does your migration...where your flock travels...take you anyplace very wet? Swampy? With standing water, maybe?"

The bird regarded her visitors for a moment, then with seeming effort, said, "Nah."

"Thank you," Vole continued, "Can you tell me...do other animals live in moisture? Wet place? In the wilds of the planet, perhaps? Far from the desert here?"

The bird's golden eyes fluttered. "Yek."

Vole nodded. "Yek? Yes? Is there any way to tell me where? I have asked the humans, and they say no such place exists."

"Vole," Vidsonnen said from behind her.

Keoka'a screeched alarmingly, throwing her head back and filling the valley with noise. She stood and stretched her wings.

"Medic Ublion," he repeated more urgently.

Vole kept eye contact with Keoka'a. "I'm sorry. It's just..."

Keoka'a flew away in a rush of red wings, screeching angrily.

"Wait!" Vole felt a hand grab her elbow and steer her into shadows. Vidsonnen's voice lost all urbane softness. "Airships, one o'clock, Medic. Take cover."

Vidsonnen pulled Vole into a narrow crevasse between halves of a cracked granite loaf. Gravel dusted her head and shoulders, making her sputter. Her mouth tasted like mud. Her scalp stung where a falling stone pinged it on the way down. Adrenaline surged through Vole, as familiar as the fear that creeping up her back. She willed it away, her senses turning sharp.

Outside, the bright valley filling with moving shadows, swooping and screaming with rage. Behind that came the sound of propellers, and then a booming. Rockets.

"Why are we hiding?" she panted. "Whoever it is wouldn't shoot people, would they?"

"They would if they didn't want witnesses." He tried to wipe his glasses clean. "You don't want them to see you, either. Third strike, you lose your license to practice medicine, isn't that what you told me?"

She rubbed her face, hands gritty. Vidsonnen stood in an alert stance, sweat running down his now dull hair, white shirt ruined. He smiled, looking like a different man.

"What are they doing? They can't be using rockets to hunt."

He craned his neck to peer outside. "I suspect they're giving looky-loos a special view of the birds. You know, *if you thought the Aviary was cool, how about disturbing a whole nesting ground?* That kind of thing is big business here."

The valley echoed with the sound of a hundred or more Jaisenets, screeching and howling angrily. A rocket whizzed and exploded, followed by a second. The ground under their feet began to rumble, gravel falling, ricocheting off the sides of the narrow space. Bullets hit stone, a dozen short pops.

The stone hallway began to rock and pitch, rocks cascading down and hitting Vole in the face. She barely avoided a long shard slicing vertically like a knife. Her elbow jarred painfully as she jumped away, eyes blinking away sand. "This isn't worth it. Let's get out of here."

"Be careful." His voice was pinched. "They don't know what they're doing. They're just...stupid opportunists...ripping off tourists."

Vidsonnen lurched forward, leaning on the wall. A narrow band of light hit a red stain blossoming across his back.

"Grigg. You've been hit."

"I noticed that too," he panted.

Vole grabbed coagulant foam from her bag and found a wide gash in the back of his head. She sprayed. "Where else are you hurt?"

"Just a few pieces of shrapnel, nothing serious," he rasped. His shirt was torn and bloody. Vole lifted it, spraying as she went. He sagged against his right shoulder, moving to sit on the ground.

"Medic Vidsonnen." She spoke loudly. "There are puncture wounds in your back. Is your lung collapsing?"

His voice was a ragged whisper. "Take the byl and run, Vole. Use your Command code. It will obey."

"Not without you." Her taeki was off grid. Vole cursed. "Stay with me. I'll flag down one of those airships. We'll get you to the Medotel."

She ripped open his shirt, revealing two large, ugly wounds, covered in white foam and blood. "I'm going to step out and get us a ride."

"Wait a second." He clutched at her tunic. "I need to tell you something."

"Make it quick." Vole tried to pry his fingers off, glad to see he had enough strength to hold her there.

"Minna was delirious when she was admitted."

"Let's elevate your feet, shall we?" Vole eased him to his side. She pressed on his wounds, making him gasp. "Tell me about Minna."

"She was in a semi-lucid state, and she kept muttering about *Zoons. Magic mountain Zoons.* She said, *Oli needs to protect their magic.* Or...something like that. It's not un...uncommon among our patients to speak of...magic."

Engines purred, further away. The airships were passing. Vole tried to pry her hem out of his clutches. "Zoons, Grigg? Minna talked about giant sentient worms? Ten Black Wizards from the children's book? With their magic well? You must have had a tough time keeping a straight face."

Vidsonnen's heart rate was dropping. The propellers grew fainter as they hovered away, leaving the valley quiet. But Vole had another idea. Karpolo.

"There could be magic Zoons anywhere in the universe, really," he rasped, "If they had a friend with a cargo ship."

"Grigg, this may hurt." Vole pushed into his back more forcefully. He grunted with pain.

"It's no use, darlin'," he whispered, his mouth opening to draw in air. "You're a good girl, you know. Special. You can't see it. But you are."

Vole wiped hair out of his face with a bloody hand. "Talk to me. What other cases are you working on?"

"Cure Minna. She's just a crazy little thing, she's got her whole life..." He coughed, then relaxed against the rock wall.

"Grigg," Vole ordered. "Come back to me."

Shale pressed painfully into Vole's knees as she tried to resuscitate him, first with her mini fib, then with her hands. From that angle, the symmetry of his reconstructed features made him look like something not-quite-human, nothing like her friend. Vole pushed away his now-limp hands, wondering what he had looked before the ship fire, what he had been like as a boy. He lay barely breathing, in a dark corridor of stone, his white shirt sticky with drying blood. Her eyes stung with the sadness and waste of it.

She hadn't felt that particular rage in years. It tasted like hot metal in her mouth, like chemicals and death.

Grigg Vidsonnen drew a final, rattling breath, and his long, slim body went still. Vole closed his eyes, whispering the words of blessing, then sat back. She drew a shaky breath, expecting panic, or battlefield numbness, to begin its work of tearing apart her psyche. But nothing happened. All Vole felt was calm, focused fury.

Her eye caught motion, a flash of silver and black. Vole stood, wiped her hands on her shirt, and walked into the valley.

Chapter Eleven

Aloft

The valley quieted, the only sound was distant airship propellers, whispering wings, and the occasional avian caw.

Vole slipped through the rock gate leading to the cliffside. Karpolo stood watching the airships float away to the south, where they rose majestically to scale a high rock formation. Her gray hair was matted, and one eye was bruised and swollen. She held her staff over one shoulder.

"Scientist Karpolo," Vole said. "Is that walking stick also a gun?"

"So what if it is? I have the right to defend my birds!" Karpolo rasped, lowering the staff. "You people have no boundaries."

"The Jaisenets are sentient." Vole moved closer. "They're not yours." Cawing erupted overhead, like a roomful of people wholeheartedly agreeing.

"They can't survive being hunted by humans. I've spent my life protecting them. I will die for them if I have to."

"Perhaps they could use protection, but they have the right to speak for themselves."

Another round of cawing.

"They're naive." Karpolo straightened, her anger incandescent. "And you know nothing. Your generation thinks only about your own species."

"You mean□*our*□own?" Vole sighed, controlling herself. "I need to use your interface. Now."

Karpolo shook her head, hair falling forward in a defeated gesture. "I destroyed it. I destroyed everything."

"I don't believe you." Vole stepped toward the cliff edge.

"It doesn't matter what you believe, Medic," the old woman said, absently pushing hair from her bruised eye, hands moving to protect her head, as Jaisenets alighted on the ground on all sides, a forest of jewel-toned feathers. Their strange, pungent odor reminded Vole of bay leaves. They made rough cooing noises. Karpolo's face grew alarmed.

"No, you can't fight them," she said to the flock, eyes wild. "They have guns, and rockets. And no shame."

The birds moved around Karpolo, but Vole could see past them. A V-shaped formation of Jaisenets rounded on the flotilla, too far away for Vole to see clearly. They divebombed the black-and-white oblong ships, striking out with long claws. Midday sun glinted off their glossy wings.

□Vole moved toward the stairs.□Karpolo pushed past the birds, sneering. "You're a human supremacist, aren't you? Your whole life's about curing us...and only us."

"I don't pimp anyone out."□

The birds cawed in agreement.

Karpolo turned. "How dare you judge me? You're nothing but a scrubbed refugee from Minth. You've lived off Authority dole your whole life."□

"Look." She pointed to the south, where the airships had come around, headed back to the nesting ground.

Karolo stepped toward her. "You don't even have a real name."

Vole's heart threatened to squeeze tight, as it always did when people saw her more clearly than she saw herself. But now she was too angry care. "Huh. I wonder how a revered public figure such as yourself got access to my secure authority file?"

"Your..." Karpolo's face betrayed her blunder. "What are you talking about?"

Vole's mind raced. "You know so much about me. That I was born on Minth. That I was an Authority ward. Even the part about my memories being scrubbed as part of my rehabilitation. I'm impressed by all the data you have access to."

Karpolo sputtered, backing toward the nesting ground. "You told me all that...when you came to my villa. You drank my hallucinatory tea."

The birds began cooing amongst themselves, a low rumble of talk. Some pawed at the ground with huge, taloned feet.

Karpolo turned. "Do you not want me to defend you?"

The airships had floated closer. Vole got her first real look at them. Rope ladders appeared from the gondolas, and incoherent shouting filled the air. The flock alighted and circled warily out over the space between the cliff edge and the plain far below.

Vole couldn't take her eyes off the ships. They were like arcane illustrations in a picture book. One had a long bandolier draped decoratively over its side, laden with bombs. Rocket launchers rotated on pendant-like emplacements. Vole felt her rage boil over. *Were those artisanal Gatlin guns? And snaking death throwers?*

"Take cover, idiot girl!" Karpolo screeched.

Vole laughed giddily as her blood ran cold; *was that a pirate flag?*

An amplified man's voice filled the air. "Stay where you are."

Vole hit the dirt between two boulders as a bomb exploded nearby. Her nostrils filled with acrid dust.

"Sorry! Are you okay? We didn't mean to do that."

The dirigibles began to collide with one another, accidentally shooting off more missiles.

"I told you to wait for my signal," the first man said in an exasperated voice.

"You signaled!"

"No, I didn't. We agreed that the thumbs up would mean don't shoot, the thumbs down would mean shoot."

A third, female voice shouted. "Nuh uh. It was the other way around..."

There was more incomprehensible shouting.

"Stop it, you imbeciles!" Karpolo yelled. "This is not a joke!"

Dozens of angry, bright green snakes roiled angrily into the light from a newly opened hole in the ground. Birds swooped in like a winged army, to feed on them.□Vole saw her chance and ran toward the cliffside.□Another explosion convulsed the ground behind her, where she had been standing. People yelled, bullets hit rocks, and birds screeched with anger. Vole let her feet slip ahead of her, her weight moving to her hips as she fell into a skid. The iron loop slid, closer, closer. At the precise right moment, she grabbed for it. Rusty metal grazed her fingertips, as she flew over the edge.□

Into thin air.

Then Vole was windmilling wildly, cold air pressing upward against her, her breath caught in terror. The cliff edge disappeared overhead, and with it the dirigibles. Vole thought about Xan's□graceful hands, the ones she never allowed herself to catch hold of, to cling to, even though he'd offered her the chance a hundred times. Her eyes filled with tears. Realization pierced her like a spike.□She was in love with Xan.□And now he would die on Lafford, sentenced by the machinations of an overzealous politician afraid of an epidemic, because Vole had failed to find Oliason,□and even worse hadn't located Sairasma's source, wherever it was on the forsaken planet that was rising up to kill her. And this knowledge filled her with sadness, not only because she had never told Xan what she felt, but because she was more afraid of her blinding need for him than she was of dying.□

Vole closed her eyes, ready for the void. But it didn't come. Without warning, Vole's body cinched and buckled, knocking the wind out of her. She gasped for air as her momentum shifted from vertical drop to horizontal glide. Her waist was held firmly, but her arms and leg floated free.□Below her, the green valley floor spun past, giving way to a landscape of sparse trees and wide, mirror-like pools.

She was alive.

And then, another, startling realization;□*she was flying*. Colorful shapes were tracking on both sides; gold, silver, purple, and teal blue.□ Wind whipped her hair in her eyes, as she strained to turn her head.□Above her, wide, crimson wings caught an updraft, and they soared higher.

At some point, when the landscape below had turned to ice and snow and her hands had grown numb, Vole closed her eyes. Jauhaa, flying to her right, cooed at her encouragingly, so she opened them again. The faintly pink air stung. She couldn't help smiling, seeing the white drifts tinted a faint candy hue, like an endless cake, below.

A huge, white-rock crater came into view, blurring the boundary between ice and the mountainside. They descended in circles, Jauhaa cawing conversationally. The three other Jaisenets answered. All seemed to agree, this was the place.

Vole collapsed in a heap on frigid stone, too numb to move. Jauhaa nudged her gently, cooing and clicking with encouragement.

"You want me to do jumping jacks?" Vole performed clumsy calisthenics until the tingling began to hurt too much. "Where are we, friend?"

Jauhaa's eye flicked to a circular indentation in the mountainside. Vole laughed. "Thank you for saving my life. But if you think I'm going in there, you're..."

Too late. With a final squawk and a rush of wings, Jauhaa took off. The four Jaisenets glided back to the south, their black shadows lurching over uneven, snowy slopes.

"No! Dammit," Vole called, without much force. Steam blossomed from her mouth. She trudged up to the indentation, swearing again as it became a tunnel, dark and wide. In twenty meters, the floor turned to slush over flat marble, and the opening's circumference grew to twice Vole's height. She began feeling warmer and noticed a pale glow. Minute sprinklings of bright blue-white fungi dusted craggy walls.

Fingers warm again, Vole checked her taeki, and decided to leave it powered down. Best be invisible for now. She wasn't in danger of freezing to death, and a thin film of icy water trickled down in places. It tasted sweet.

The light brightened as Vole trudged deeper into the tunnel, sloping gradually up to what she thought was the west. As she moved along, a strange odor began to permeate the air, musky and metallic, a bit like blood but more pungent. Something was there, in the dark circle ahead. Something alive.

The thing Jauhaa wanted Vole to see.

She drank some water from her bag, checking her sample kit. Her meds were in their deep pocket, but Vole had no desire to use any. A sucking sound echoed in the tunnel. For the first time since escaping the airships, Vole felt afraid. She had no weapons. No one knew where she was. One of her worst fears, enclosure, should have been triggered the moment she stepped inside the cave. But curiosity overrode all that.

"Hello?"

Light burst forth, blinding her temporarily. A string of blue-flame lanterns appeared, unlike anything she had seen before. She walked more quickly now. Dark lichen grew under her feet, and the air turned humid.

After twenty minutes, Vole entered a vast cave of glittering crystals, with a placid central lake. Dark, tubular shapes lay in rows, like a clinic supply drawer, only these were huge. She stepped forward.

The tubes reared up with a sucking sound, revealing faces, at least a hundred of them. Vole gasped. There had been stories told in Medic journos of legendary Ertsu Zoons, sentient creatures who had abandoned modernity and space travel for a simple life underground. What had the rumors said? Only that they chose to be zoons, but could change their shapes if they wanted to. Being zoons was a spiritual practice for them.

Each Ertsu was as long as ten men, and twice as wide. Their features were blunt, with minute noses and large, childlike eyes. Their skin, not really black on closer inspection, but a shimmering shade of graphite, stretched into smiles, revealing two wide, white ridges that must serve as teeth. Vole knew as a scientist that she shouldn't anthropomorphize alien creatures. But...they were adorable. She burst into nervous laughter.

A hundred mouths joined in her merriment.

She fainted.

Chapter Twelve

Precious

The creatures' snake-like graphite skin rippled. They lay tangled up in one another, so she couldn't tell how long they were, but each was as thick as she was tall. Vole waited for one of them to wrap itself around her, strike out with fangs, or worse. Long, tense seconds passed.

Water drops rippled out on the lake's glimmering blue-black surface, circles meeting and dissolving in a constant pattern. Her ragged breathing echoed, over loud. The air smelled something like yeast in sugar water, warm and alive. She had no idea where that memory came from. Courage appeared, though, like a flame in her mind.

"Whoever you are," Vole whispered. "Can you speak to me? I'm having some trouble. And I...I need help."

The landscape shifted suddenly, a looming presence that made her jump. Two dozen dark gray creatures reared up like cobras, their bodies unsticking from one another with a roar of suction. Vole gasped, staring up at them, at their...*faces*, she gulped, tears running down her face. *Faces,* almost human, intelligent and calm, with no trace of aggression. Foreign though they were, she understood that she was not going to be eaten. At least, not immediately.

Though, what were they thinking, these...not exactly people, but something not too far distant, either? Beings. The worm-like people were obviously sentient, staring into her face with wide, wondrous eyes. Her terror shifted to curiosity. What could these beings conclude by her presence?

"Excuse me if I'm trespassing," Vole said. She made a bow of universal respect, then sagged to her knees and waited.

They gazed down on her with expressions of benign interest, their large, flat heads swaying slightly.

A pair of words appeared in Vole's mind, slipping into place like pieces of a puzzle. *Erstu Zoons*. Zoons, just as Vidsonnen had said, his final muttered thought. A creature that, while elusive, was recorded in the annals of biology. Megafauna, endangered, perhaps? She couldn't remember. But definitely famous, from children's stories, religious fables, and obscene cartoons.

They were far scarier in real life, yet instinct told her not to jump to conclusions. *Her mind had done that far too much*, a voice inside whispered. She had lost some ability, the clarity of vision a scientist needed in order to learn. Her breathing settled a little.

"Hello." she muttered.

A dozen large eyes gazed at her. The creatures' human-like faces must be one reason illustrators liked to paint them, Vole thought; flat noses, puffy cheeks, and wide, expressive mouths. Despite their twenty-meter length and five-meter circumference, they were adorable.

The Zoons smiled at Vole, and she smiled back, panic and excitement warring in her chest. She searched her memory for anything about them. She knew, though she didn't recall where she had learned it, that the Ertsu Zoons had abandoned modernity and space travel for a simple life underground. *What had the fables said?* Only that taking the form of a humble Zoon was a spiritual experience for them, a way to let go of their previous material encumbrances and expand their consciousness. They were alchemists, altering their own DNA. This worm-form was a choice.□

A strange sound bubbled between the stalactites and stalagmites, and Vole realized it was her own laughter. The Zoons smiled again, and made noises like wind in bottles, a tuneless, resonant song. The lake rippled in the semi-darkness, causing the whole cave to sparkle.

"I'm Vole," she gestured.

They made more flute-like noises, and she laughed. Two dozen mouths replied, making a chorus of voices so varied and magnificent that the cavern became a cathedral. One of the Zoons put its face up to Vole's, as if to kiss her. She braced herself, but instead of a pair of worm lips, she felt the touch of something wet on her mouth, a drop of cool, sweet water. She gulped it thirstily.

A pooling creek flowed over quartz banks, a meter away. Vole went to it, scooping its fresh, icy water into her parched mouth. Then she lay down on the hard ground, gazing up at the jagged ceiling with its places of shadow and light. She felt exhausted, not only her mind but her body, which had begun to glow with warmth. Tension oozed from her muscles. Her breathing deepened. She let her lids drift closed.

In blackness now, she was neither asleep, nor awake. She was merely alive. A fizzing sound drew her attention to her chest. She saw with fascination that where her heart ought to be, a fist-sized sparkle burned, sending sparks in all directions, making lines that stretched into infinity, then faded, over and over. Vole found this situation mildly surprising, especially when she realized that the thing in her chest had always been there. She had just never noticed it, beaming away like a ball of fire. What a thing to miss. Vole studied the flame, dispassionately, as she would a campfire on a quiet night. It was beautiful, incandescent white, alive with movement, yet no bigger than her head at the tip of its widest ray.

The fireball fizzed with a sharp and steady glow. The fizzing sounded familiar to Vole, like the memory of something. She had the feeling of the minute star in her chest being connected to all stars, in all galaxies, and the noise it made being nothing more than particles of cosmic dust shooting past.□

Vole considered the pink sky of Bilioth, and the auroras of Minth, the orbits of all planets, in all solar systems; the dance of all matter, in the whole, immense universe. Every movement pointed toward life, against all odds, despite the coldness and indifference of the vast cavity of space. The tiniest amoeba was a miracle.□

Vole smiled to herself, in the dark space, knowing she was part of that infinite, celestial tide; every cell in her, every broken and functional part. She was one with all of it. She regarded the sizzling light that was her heart, her real one, not the muscle that valiantly pumped blood through her flesh, but the essential her, the thing that was neither alive nor dead, but simply was. And as she watched, something in Vole released, some deep and stubborn truth that had been stuck there. She was free to let it go. She had never been trapped, not really.

And Vole Ublion realized that she would never be truly afraid again.

And then Vole woke, in the cave, in her now-naked body. Time had passed.

Her first feeling was comfort, warmth, and peace. She was cushioned in a cocoon. She couldn't remember ever feeling better. She opened her eyes and saw without emotion that she was enveloped in a pocket of Zoon flesh, which cradled her gently.

She rolled on one side to study the lake, and the warm pocket shifted like a sleeping bag. She noted with mild surprise that her gut no longer held a dark box of danger. She was clean inside. She started to laugh. Vole understood in that moment that she was very high. Stoned, but not out of her mind.□

The Zoons whistled a low chord, welcoming her. She whistled back, and they all laughed. Vole knew what they were doing. She had come to them shivering and covered in blood. Forces were against her, but she had stopped asking why. Her will was worn to a single track;□*duty, responsibility, and sacrifice.* She could not keep up the pace. The wise worms understood that her light, her essential self, was drowning in darkness.

How long had this been so?

Vole saw for the first time that this state of being was wrong. She was precious, not to the Zoons, but to the universe. As if from a safe distance, she saw herself trying to hide in the business of people's bodies, their pain and suffering. She swam in it, her own sorrow stirred into the larger stew until she felt the reassuring distraction of selflessness. As long as she was nothing but Medic Ublion, her life disappeared into the larger swirl, where she didn't know her own flavor, and didn't have energy to care.

The Zoons had given her something rare and good. Vole couldn't name it, but she hoped they'd share the recipe. She'd taken meds for years. But nothing had allowed her to stand outside of her life, and see, not like this, the way she would a patient, with all her skill and knowledge. Vole Ublion was a wreck.□

Yet, the wise beings holding her now believed she could be salvaged. She relaxed with a sigh. If not for Xan, she wasn't sure she was concerned about living through the experience. She was so tired, so very tired of the struggle. As soon as she had that thought, it seemed to spin out of her like a thread of smoke, or of ectoplasm. She watched it unwind into the crystalline air above her, beyond the muscular worm flanks, and disappear into the ethos. How strange. She felt lighter, without that dark weight. She had thought it was hers to carry forever, but now it was gone.

Vole unclenched her hands, unfolding her body, feeling again her legs, her toes, her shoulders and back. Her reason for being there fluttered into her mind, softly, the slightest bit surprising because she'd all but forgotten it. Oliason, and Sairasma, and a quarantine on Waystation Lafford. She tried to muster the motivation to ask the Zoons. But what they were teaching her was something more important. The birds had known they would.□

Vole studied the cavern, the slow dripping of water, which she now understood had been chemically altered, in some way she didn't grasp but that had to do with the Zoons' physiology. Their alchemy was one of habitation, of bending their environment to their task. This place was holy, a shrine to the oneness of all things. It was also a very potent chemical mix, a cauldron of consciousness.

Jauhaa had trusted Vole to protect it. But why? Vole replayed her interactions with the birds.□*What was the link between the Jaisenets and the Ertsu Zoons?*□For a moment a bright thread appeared in her mind; the link, the logical cohesion. Then it darted away. She chased it, the elusive truth about why she had been brought here.

A smell-sight-sound moved through her, synesthetic music, a musk rainbow, melting and folding in vivid hues, a tincture of promise. Her laughter echoed in the still air.□*Command Medic Vole Ublion*□, she said to herself,□*compose yourself.* The scientist in her yearned to understand what the Zoons had concocted. Because it was good, more than good. It was beautiful.□A voice that came from everywhere at once said,□*remember your dream.*

A feeling ran up her legs, like soft flames melting away a tightly wrapped binding, leaving her unscathed, freed, exhilarated. Vole felt the sweet relief of it. She had been so deeply asleep, leagues under, swimming where she might have lost her breath. Memory loosened, then spread, the way a leaf suddenly unfolds, knowing where to hold itself in the light.

Remember.

Chapter Thirteen

The Past is Another Planet

Time collapsed in on itself in perfect, vivid detail.□Vole's whole life was suddenly alive within her, a switch flipped from inert to active.

Remember

Vole's opaque, mysterious past expanded in complete detail, painful but tolerable. She unfolded the darkness she had clutched around herself like a cloak, and with it of the effort to hold it tightly bound for so long. She stepped forth, vulnerable and unarmed.□ But the part of her that always rose up to grab at safety didn't stir. A bright cacophony of sound and feeling rushed around her, the bottom of a wave. She steadied herself with a hand on the nearest Zoon's solid flank, leaning her face against its comforting warmth.□

Remember.

First, she was small, eight or nine years old, on her home planet of Minth. Their house was high in a cubiconset, cramped and leaky. The faces of her parents, siblings, and extended relatives peered down at her, their bones and skin a variation on her own. The group felt complete; her people, her own kind, those who carried her in their hearts. Children, old folks, those the age she was and younger. Her tribe, troubled and desperate. Someone smoothed her hair, smiling a white-toothed smile. A woman, dark green eyes and furrowed brow, a gentle touch from which Vole had no impulse to flinch away.□*Mommin.*□Her own Mommin. Vole had had a mother. She studied this fact dispassionately, unable to stop and feel the weight of it just then. There was so much more to recall.□

Memory shifted forward. Now they were on a spaceship, and Mommin was crying. Vole was tired of the place, of feeling constrained, of keeping still.□*Amther* was there, too, her own big father; handsome face contorted with worry, beard wet with tears. They were so young, her parents, hardly more than children themselves. Amther was yelling into the network, and someone over the interface replied in a stern tone. They were in trouble. An Authority Air Guard was warning their ship;□*their credentials were obvious forgeries. Planetary access was denied. To avoid disciplinary action, they were to leave exosphere immediately and return to Minth.*

The adults spoke words of planning, of calculation; Vole remembered their gruff, utilitarian Minthan, the show of calloused, worker's hands when they voted on a course of action. One woman screamed that□*they were making a mistake, that they could go home,* but she was rebuffed with arguments;□*they had no money, their ship was stolen, and they'd surely be put to death for the crime.* A hyperventilating man shouted that□*the children's future was not worth risking all their lives,* but others quieted him, telling him he should have thought of that long before. It was too late to abort the plan. Vole smelled their sweat and desperation, and the sharp-bitter tang of hope.

Heads bowed in concentration, ten or twelve of them. Someone called out that they needed to hurry. The ship's interior flashed and flamed as systems went offline, first the Velraen consoles, then the Com array. Her lungs stung with acrid poison as the air filled with smoke.□

Gravity set in, and she could feel that their ship was plunging down. The passengers pressed together, silent but for a couple of sobbing children. Vole was suffocating, her ribs crushed. People prayed in soft voices. Her tears fell onto Amther's dirty shirt.

In memory, the deafening rip of an explosion frightened her. The bubble lit up with flashes, from outside, the heat shields disintegrating. She craned her neck to see flaming debris falling to a mottled gray planet, its watery plain pressing down onto their ship, eating them.□

They began to shimmy sickeningly. People screamed, and their terror tore over her, like fire. Screaming, wordless and horrible.

How could she have forgotten this?□

But she knew. The Authority had ways. Command had ways. Someone had worked hard on her, to suppress this trauma. She breathed it out, summoning the courage that seemed to burn as brightly as before. Vole pressed her face into the snake-smooth side of a Zoon, and walked back into memory.□

The air was boiling. Vole was being murdered. Her feet were burning off, someone's hair was flaming; was it hers? The smell made her choke. Adults pressed against her with their bodies, too hard, the contents of their stomachs covering her. Her lungs were bursting.

The memory was horrific. But it didn't kill her, nor the sparkling life in her chest. Vole felt sad, and raw, and real. She breathed slowly, letting the memories settle.□

A droplet of water hit the surface of the lake, spreading and growing, like her mind. There was more. Much more. Perhaps too much. Vole resolved to see it all. If the Zoons' chemical protection couldn't keep her safe, then she was fine to die there. But she needed to know herself, first.

The escape pod's lurching had stopped. The silent ship plummeted, down and down and down. Her face was stretched, her family pulled from her. She fainted.

Then young Vole was in empty space. She forced air into her lungs, but it hurt to breathe. She whispered. No one answered. She pushed the junk that was crushing her away, not looking at it, not seeing the bodies of her family, though she knew they were there. The dead flesh was no one, nothing; her family would come soon, and all of this would be a dream. Mommin would sing. Amther would carry her to the hammocks. This was only a nightmare.

Vole crawled toward a water smell, green slime marbling a black pool. She drank, then wretched, then lay with her face on wet grass, crying until sleep took her. When she woke, voices were babbling incomprehensibly. The language was a strange, dissonant song. Vole understood by the strangers' blank faces that her people were dead and could give nothing.

Vole was dead, too, of course. Only her body kept living. When they saw her, the incomprehensible ones pushed her with their feet. They spoke about her in bored voices. They picked her body up without gentleness. She was an empty sack.

Vole said nothing. She felt nothing. A man put her on the back of a creature, who craned its head and tried to bite her. Vole cringed, crying out, and her head exploded with a blow from the man's stick. She trembled as the man then hit the animal's head, twice. They began to move. The sun went down, and the blue-and-green world went black.□

The next thing she remembered was being stripped naked, made to stand under a blinding light, before a crowd of people. The man with the beast called out to the audience, and someone answered rudely. In this way, she learned the man's name; Zjoah. He hit Vole again, trying to get her to stand taller. But she was shivering, and afraid. The crowd heckled.

Zjoah took her back to his village. A woman looked at Vole with hard eyes and made a gesture of damnation. Next Vole smelled dirt. She sat in a dark place, shivering, hungry. Sun crept over the village, but did not reach Vole. She was under a sturdy wooden grid, in a dirt hole, several meters deep. She found an ancient tunic that smelled of mildew and spiders. She pulled it over her and waited.

Vole became very good at waiting. That was the time in her life when boredom and hunger were her friends; they meant that the Villagers had forgotten about her. Those moments were always too short.□

When she ate, it meant Zjoah was taking her up to the terrible place. She longed to die, then, and return to her people. But she did not die. She envied her ancestors their deaths. She cursed the sky over her head, who had killed everyone but her. She cried silently, asking what she had done to be so punished.□

The Vole in the cave, watching, knew that in these years, just before the war, the Vel.1s had cut off shipments of food to much of the diaspora. The Human Race was realizing, with growing horror, that Singularity had come. It was a time of terrible suffering. Vole became an animal, itching and bruised, burning with sores. The village was a place of dirt and darkness. Men pulled her up on ropes. At first, they took her behind hillocks or huts to use her body, looking around to be sure they weren't seen. She didn't struggle, didn't cry, couldn't force herself to say the words they tried to make her say. They hit her in frustration, but she would not speak.

Strangers came to the village. Vole heard them through branches that were thrown across her pit, to hide it. Men yelled, and women shrieked. The smell of smoke was dank and sweet. The Villagers muttered prayers. One woman came and pissed down Vole's wall. The woman spoke, so Vole raised her eyes. She was surprised when the woman withdrew, in fear.

Then came nights of bonfires. The men dragged her from her hole, and did the things they had once been ashamed of, now in view of the whole village. There were few people now. They laughed, their eyes livid in firelight. The children watched, at first amazed. Then, the children began to help. They hit her, jeering at her in words she had no energy to hear. But it was no use. Vole had no tears to give them. She was a body with no soul. Vole fell into the night's velvet blackness. She begged the sky to kill her, as it had killed her family.□

She began to black out. Dawn brought in pain from deep knife cuts in her skin.□ She ached, always. Each night, she was broken again. The nights all collapsed together.

Sometimes in her hole, when the cold crept in and turned her limbs turned blue, then fever showed planets colliding, exploding with silent flashes, Vole believed the sky was taking pity on her and calling her home. So many times, she grew strong again, and found herself scratching for bugs. She stopped praying for mercy. Rodents crawled onto her shoulders, nibbling at her matted hair.□ *Voles*, the smallest and most insignificant of mice, were her only friends. They showed her care, licking the blood from her wounds. Biting, to remind her she was still alive. Vole was nothing then, but the thirst, and the hunger, and the pain.

She startled herself, back in the cave, the sound of her own sobbing echoing through the hall of crystals, like a hundred ghosts theatrically booing. It made her laugh, through her tears. Vole didn't want to stop.

The relief of it was too sweet, the feeling of lightness and emptiness. She would cry and cry, until the nothingness was all out.

She leaned her head on a dark, muscular flank, and let memory come.

In the village, Vole waited with the other Voles, eating scraps, drinking rain, until the season of bonfires came again. She understood by then that the villagers were starving. They were keeping her, hoping for her to ripen, so they could take her back to the marketplace. But that day would never come. Vole was as ugly as a dying sapling. No one would want her. The woman came back to piss, many times. In memory, Vole saw the fear in her, the desperation. The woman hated Vole, because of how they had treated her. It made the village vulnerable, to the gods, to the law. She saw now the rage of a mother who could not feed her children and needed someone to blame.

Vole did not forgive, nor did she feel the need to. But she saw. She saw ordinary, human evil. Was it any wonder the Vel.1s had tried to eliminate their species?

The next chapter of Vole's life appeared without warning. There was a morning of loud sirens, on land and in the sky, and amplified words, from what she now knew were Authority Terrabyls and Enforcement Cruisers. Then gunfire came, and more words. Villagers screamed, as some were killed, and others caught.

Hands ripped open the top of Vole's cage. Hands reached and pulled her body out, arms too long to be human. She saw the village for the first time in daylight, the debris-strewn huts, men standing with pitchforks, holding slingshots, their faces terrified. She understood the people's language then. But she made no effort to listen to their begging.

Velraen android soldiers walked deliberately, like monsters, sprouting six arms each, faces flat gray masks. Vole was not afraid. She asked if they had come to kill her.

"Miss, you are the victim of multiple crimes. Please wait here while we carry out justice."

They put her up into an armored Terrabyl, where she sat behind glass, watching. The soldiers began shooting.

The vehicle's interface spoke softly to her, about the law, about the grid. "What is your name?"

"I don't know," she croaked. "How did you find me?"

"Anomalies were detected by satellite."

Vole smiled. The sky had seen her. It had heard her prayers.

"Miss. Please hold still," the interface said, as robot arms took hold of her. She felt a needle prick, as they put her into stasis.

Vole awoke from stasis, in a body that had grown, with long brown hair, and strength in her muscles. She watched in fascination as Med-Gens erased scars on her forearms, answering all her questions as they carefully anesthetized, smoothing the cuts. The gashes on her legs were too deep to erase without more surgeries, they said. She did not mind the touch of machines. They said soothingly,□*one day we will repair the underlying cause of this crime.*□Even after they became her enemy, she wished she could be more like the gray people who killed, and healed, with equal clarity.

Vole's memory shifted ahead to a Vel.1 on the orphanage waystation. The android, who said its' name was□*Teacher*, demonstrated the use of a spork, and explained how to turn out the lights in the dormitory cubicles. The waystation slowly filled with other kids, like her, traumatized and savage from hiding from the war. The Vel.1 instructors were infinitely patient, calm and all-knowing. They were kind to Vole, who had no concept of kindness. At first, she hid in small, secret places, but they always found her, coaxing her out with logical explanations until she grew bored and crawled out. Twice, she tried to attack them and escape, but the androids were powerful and lightning-fast, holding her aloft in a firm grip while she screamed and raged. They never punished her or said harsh words. They encouraged her to run on the treadmill, play with animals in the therapy class-rooms, and when her comprehension improved, to be read to by the interface. She didn't remember the precise moment she turned back into a human girl. Vole could not have asked for a kinder team. It was treason to think it but she did; they were perfect beings, this class of android, the Vel. 1s, who became sentient. Who became killers

No one ever explained why their programming divided humans into enemy combatants and regular clients. Over time, Vole came to understand it had to do with being registered in the system. Anyone without a recorded identity was invisible. Everyone else, all those who had profiles in any database throughout the diaspora, was hunted. It was why data collection had been outlawed in the armistice treaty. Vole was an illegal alien, a citizen of nowhere, her birth unrecorded, her life untraceable. Her lack of identity did nothing to trigger the Vel. 1s' programming. So, she was saved, tended to, and protected from the war on a base far from Earth, where battles raged, and people were exterminated in the millions.

Ordinary memories spooled past, unremarkable, familiar. Vole, in school, answering questions in class. Studying for finals in the library. Vel.1s in front of the classroom, speaking about mathematics and biology. She grew big. She learned, and feared no testing. She ate and slept alongside many other orphans like her.

Then one day, as the children watched, their machine instructors stood up straight, and their red eyes grew distant, as if hearing a call from far away. They turned, then moved in perfect unison, their matte gray figures walking softly out the door and down the hallway.

The students never saw them again. Humans took their places, explaining that the Vel.1s were their mortal enemies. None of the androids were safe. None were to be trusted. *All future helper machines would be called Vel.2s, and they would always be distinguishable from the enemy, because now it was unlawful to build robots in human form.*

Vole had thought: *no one could mistake them for human.* Their skin was flat gray, and they were strong, and they had saved her from humans, who were imperfect and weak, and prone to do terrible things. Why should not the machines inherit the universe?

Vole thought then that the human race was doomed. She had seen what Vel.1 soldiers could do, their skill in battle, their imperviousness to harm. But she said nothing. She owed them her life, and if they wanted it back, the machines could take it. It was then that she decided to become a helper, not a combatant. If she was stuck in a human body, she knew better than to fight Velraens. She wished more than anything that she could be more like them; perfect, hard, and clever.

The waystation moved to orbit a white planet they nicknamed *Snowball.* Its real name was 90800, a silver-white orb shimmering below them, frozen seas crackling with blue lightning. Dogfights. Bombardments. The enemy had tried to hide deep under an ice cap, but the humans were rooting them out. The students were told to be proud of this victory. But Vole felt only sorrow.

They were given new lessons, in combat and strategy, firearms and fitness. They took batteries of tests. Vole was unafraid of blood during first-aid training. She did not cry when another child slashed her leg with errant laser fire. She remained calm when the station was bombed, and then evacuated. Her supervisors said Vole was lucky. She would be given a special assignment, fit only for people like her, who had no feelings.

For the first time in her life, Vole got the thing she wanted; Medic training. She couldn't learn fast enough; the intricacies of bodies, chemical interactions in the blood, the treatment of wounds both physical and psychic. Vole worked hard. She was like everyone else, then, just another refugee with an uncertain future, trying to survive.□

Then in the locker room after an intense autopsy, another trainee kissed her lips. Vole backed away. The panic, always a seed in her heart, exploded. She curled in a ball, shivering and nauseous. Instructors arrived, calm and efficient, and whispered that□*she was not the only one.*

Vole asked,□*what is wrong with me?*

They said,□*you are being hunted, and you know it. Try to forget. Or at least pretend. So the others can carry on.*

She took the meds and recovered. Graduation came; Vole's first sip of whiskey, in a borrowed dress. She danced with friends; gloves on, moving with the music. Their eyes found her legs, the tree-bark skin, slashed and torn. Pitying eyes, whispers, the others suddenly saw what Vole was.□

She took too many meds after that, and had to have her stomach pumped.□*If it weren't wartime, we'd have to expel you,*□they said.

But they were at war, living in tent cities on obscure planets, their skies lit up by fire. Vole's first day as a Medic, on hellaciously hot planet 80775, was a blur of blood and gore, waves of broken people that just kept coming. Her ears closed to all but the sounds she chose to hear, her eyes focused on the body on the gurney in front of her, her gloved hands moving quickly, never stopping to think. She was good at this, at choosing what to know, and what to forget.

On the tenth day without rest, Vole collapsed in the middle of surgery. She woke on a gurney, her scrubs covered with offal, stinking, her feet still in rubber shoes. She staggered into a sweltering twilight, dehydrated, and hungry. The sky seemed to be laughing. Stars twinkled down at her, their jagged light so similar to a Vel.1 attack cruiser, no one would be able to tell the difference, until the missiles came.□

She stood at the door to the mess hall, unable to enter. It was full of people, living in a world of hope, and belief. Vole was not like them. In her heart, Vole was a Velraen.1, from before the Singularity, just a machine that looked human. An automaton.□

From that moment on, Vole didn't like being around people. The thought of their fragile bodies, their vulnerable minds, the overwhelming needs they threw around carelessly, that she was too weak and limited to meet.□Did she look like such a one, to the Zoons?

Chapter Fourteen

A Shot in the Dark

There was something more, a spot on the sparkling, tiny sun in her chest, a dampening. Vole wanted it out, the unexamined thing, whatever it was. The piece of herself she had forgotten, or been made to forget. It felt wrong to keep it where it was, blocking the light.

Vole scooped water from the cool lake with her hands, letting it run down her cheeks and onto her skin. The taste was faintly medicinal, but mostly mineral, pleasant and fresh. She made a note to herself that if she ever got out of there, she would use the vials in her bag to bring some of it back for testing. But the Zoons' wizardry was washing through her body now. She crept back to her perch on the stones, the closest Zoon curved around like a protective berm, and closed her eyes.

Remember.

She gasped with recognition. The attack. Her record showed she had been a supervisor, that much she knew. She had some visuals with the knowledge; stock pictures, she realized in the cave. Generic clinic imagery, most likely, implanted during therapeutic protocols.

What she remembered now was shatteringly specific. With full sensory detail, Vole was back in the clinic on Planet 33439. She'd been a full field clinic Administrator. Her facility was surrounded by water, complex tides and currents ripping through reeds below their stilts. Staff were forever coping with insects, snakes and lizards, which turned up everywhere, even the operating rooms, while Vole was suturing shrapnel wounds and cleaning combat burns. But the place was relatively quiet.

Oh yes. 33439 was a considered good place for Humans, because Velraens were vulnerable to water.

The clinic had been there long enough that the locals paddled their small boats there for ordinary care. They paid her in dried fish and amber trinkets, and pickled mammal fat. She liked being responsible. It was the closest Vole had ever been to happy.

The skirmish came late in the war. The enemy was on the run, its few remaining strongholds mostly on Earth. The humans were hopeful, their past losses so staggering they had little left to lose, tactics growing more effective as they adapted to the new reality. Planets were being abandoned, colonies consolidated. The Authority drew up the new quadrants to reflect a spartan, dissipated populace. The Quadrant Forum was established to govern what they hoped would one day be a renewed civilization. The Declaration of Peace was being drawn up and debated, still a long way from being ratified, but still.□*Peace*, the journos said,□*was on the horizon.*

Vole saw the contest as purely one of power; and in that struggle, she had learned, life always won. The Vel.1s had no fear of death, as they were only machines; what they hated was the creeping, endless force that would always cause them chaos; nature. Spores, seeds, the stuff of new life that no amount of sterilizing could destroy. What won the war wasn't combat, but mold, compost, organic material; only in Space were the Velraens free of its influence, and they didn't care about Space. They wanted a planet. Even though the planet would eventually kill them.

Vole was in a plumb spot, watching the wind in the swampy trees, joking with the water people, sending soldiers back to their units with an admonition to keep out of harm's way just long enough for the Authority to negotiate a settlement.

The patrol came at night. Clinics had nothing to use against rockets and automatic guns. They were supposed to be neutral places, unthreatening and not worth destroying. Apparently, that had changed. The enemy was growing desperate.

Vole heard the ships across the sound, and sent her staff away, into the swampy forest where they would have cover. They took with them two wounded soldiers, one unconscious, dragged on a line, the other with ruined legs, but arms strong enough to row. The clinic's two steadiest Gens, a man and a woman, stayed behind with her. They had talked about their plan in advance. But it was still reckless, and Vole hoped, unexpected.

As a swarm of armed Vel.1 drones swooped down toward them, Vole and her people set the empty clinic on fire. The heat signatures would draw missile fire, and buy a bit of time.

Then six Vel.1 gunships were on them, cyclonic propellers whipping spray all around the stilted facility, a sudden squall. The noise was deafening. Vole and the two Gens moved to the shelter of some scrubby shrubs on a sand bank. Each of them carried a case of flares. There was no point in signaling for help; human fighter planes were too precious to waste on a lost cause, and the clinic was definitely lost, red-orange flames licking into the night sky, the whipped-up rain doing little to dampen the blaze.

Vole signaled for the Gens to stop. They loaded their flare rifles, careful to keep the boxes dry, stuffing extras in pouches and pockets. The Vel.1s called in their drones, then hovered into a circular formation, around the clinic, waiting for anyone still inside to flee, so they could pick them off. Velraens didn't give up easily, making little distinction between types of human being. They wanted them all dead. But, Vole suspected, they would abandon their attack when the building collapsed, and go hunting for the survivors.

After that, they would go looking for the main army. The Vel.1s had long since figured out that field clinics were always within an hour's reach of the front. Vole didn't know the exact location of the ten-thousand-odd cluster of soldiers and staff, only that it was somewhere to the south. But if the gunships started sweeping, as they were likely to, they'd find it by morning.

Vole waded into the cool, hip-high water. Grasses flowed around her legs, their roots a tangle she had to step over carefully to keep her flare gun dry. The gunships hovered twenty yards away, five or six meters off the water, propellers neatly tucked into their horizontal position. It would be easier if they turned to vertical, but horizontal meant they were still waiting.

Her feet found a flat place in the reeds, and she took a warrior stance, raising the rifle to her shoulder. Waves rippled around her hips. She blinked as a part of her clinic sheared off and fell smoking into the water. Her mind went very clear. There were still stars above her, but the horizon had brightened, and between the coming sunrise and her now-engulfed clinic, she saw every detail; the ships, the propellers, the metal-and-resin legs of Velraen men, dangling half out of the ships, waiting to pick off anyone they could.

Vole took aim and shot. The flare exploded, meeting propeller, shredding into a swirl of angry sparks. The cyclone slowed and sputtered, expelling the broken flare. She smiled. She aimed and shot, aimed and shot, the rifle butt bucking painfully into her shoulder, stopping only to reload. The sound of flames was drowned out as one of the propellers caught, wheezing with anger, then exploded. A gunship guttered as it fell, flaming, into the silvery water, which hissed and steamed. Two others tried to fly away, one falling quickly, the other spinning sickeningly until it smashed through the water.

Vole kept firing, moving now, sure they would come after her. Hoping, with a small smile of reckless mirth, that they would. Two of the ships were in trouble, one rising high on its one remaining propeller, the other wobbling like a poorly spun top. The two healthy gunships lowered their propellers to vertical, and moved toward her, following her heat.

That was when Vole noticed the debris floating around her, smoke rising in ribbons. Pieces of the clinic were being carried by the current into deeper water. And someone, her Gens no doubt, had set alight boxes of flares, which shot around like fireworks, in all directions. Vole ducked as one whizzed by her head, leaving a smell of Sulphur. She reloaded.

A gray man fell, and then another, and then another. They bailed out of their transport, falling through the sky to the surface, their red eyes staring at her as they rained down into the sea.

Vole ran to the place under the trees, pulling her legs up under her, afraid, watching for red lights below the surface. Though until the cave, she had not felt the strange pain of killing the Vel.1s. It had been the matte-skinned, powerful gray soldiers who rescued her from the hole in the village. They had saved her, and she had destroyed them, many of them.

What was she?

A name floated into her mind; Kaaki. Kaaki Kurtsonni. She had been named, once, been part of a family, been loved in the ordinary human way. She killed Velraens because she was alive. And life wanted only to continue, to spread and grow and make more of itself. She was broken, but she contained that spark, and survival was her destiny. Life demanded it. Her life, the flare that was in her, as important as any other.

In the morning, Vole and her Gens were picked up by a rescue transport, and off-lifted. She was given a bath, a warm meal, and a commendation, then put into stasis. They told her, when she awoke, the war would be over. And it was. Here was where her memory returned to what she had known before. The two roads converged into the moment she awoke aboard Lafford Waystation. Like so many others, Vole Ublion was detached from a stasis pod when personnel were needed for the post-war rebuild.

Mars had been the decisive victory. But Earth, the cradle of humanity, had been the treasure sacrificed. It was Vel.1 territory now, for as long as the gray people continued to operate.

The thing had been done to her, to her brain, her memory, herself. Post-traumatic Stress Protocols. The thing that the gray creatures all around her had needed only what—hours? Days? To undo.

Broken, scarred, and deeply confused, Vole whistled to the Zoons. They whistled back. She didn't know their language, but she thought they understood. She was thanking them.

Chapter Fifteen

Oliason

Vole woke in the sparkle-dark of the cavern, feeling stone cold sober, wondering what Xan must be thinking. The desire to see him was a need, now, as acute and irresistible as the hunger in her belly.

She tumbled out of the pile of Zoons, her skin goose-pimpling in the air. The ground felt smooth against her bare feet, glazed with old mineral deposits. She walked in a slow ellipse, coming back into her body, breathing the faint smell of moss. She could see clearly now that the open doorway was not a wormhole, but a built structure, girded by metal, rimmed with strange glyphs. Her friends the Zoons had been people, once. Clever biologists, no doubt, capable of manipulating their own DNA. How humble a form they had chosen.

She skipped a stone over the lake, watched the thin, silver circles expand and merge in the blackish-green mirror. Something smooth gleamed from below. Vole reached into the frigid water to where the thing lay cradled by a sandy bed of grass. Her fingers touched resin, and she pulled up a headlamp, with a thick elastic strap. She snapped it on, shining the light beam around the lake floor with its undulating weeds and tiny, transparent crustaceans, which danced away like fairies.

Vole waded into the water, gasping with cold. She dived and swam. Next to a boulder, in a thicket of black vegetation, the lamp shone on what she was looking for; the naked, pale figure of Bo Oliason, as solid and serene as a sculpture. She took his hand, and his body floated easily behind her.

Vole pulled Oliason's body to rest in a shallow crook. He was perfectly preserved, skin like marble, eyes closed in a serene face.

"You were right to protect this place, Commander. You figured no one else would ever find it. No pirates exploiting the Zoons. No so-called scientists selling them out to the highest bidder." she whispered to him. "I'll make sure this place remains secret. I promise."

Vole went to where her clothing and bag lay in a heap. She felt around in her supplies, located the kit she'd packed on Lafford, and took a sample from Oliason's lifeless arm. The Sairasma rash was painless now. He had died at peace. She silently mouthed the memorial prayer, then let him slip gently back under the surface.

"Rest in peace, Daredevil."

The Zoons rose in unison, two dozen graphite-gray, human-faced worms whistling a dirge. When it was over, the closest of them moved in, smiling, eyes flicking from Vole to the open door.

"I understand," Vole said, stroking the face with her hand. "I will try to keep the humans away. We are such a broken race. Oliason and I are not the only ones who would come here, looking for what you have."

The Zoon offered a muscular coil. Vole gently took a blood sample.

"Thank you." She kissed the Zoon's cheek. "Perhaps I can find a way to help them, with your medicine. Is that all right?"

The Zoon's head bobbed in affirmation.

Vole took three vials of water from the lake. Then she donned her clothing and shoes and shouldered her bag. She turned and gave a last whistle. Soft bottle-neck tones answered. "Goodbye, my friends." Her tears fell hot on her cheeks, but nothing dark loomed underneath, no pending attack.

Vole felt as light and unencumbered as a bird in flight.

The blue-lit tunnel seemed longer on the way up, winding and circling. She rummaged in her bag, finding a bottle of water from Vidsonnen's Leona, which she gulped thirstily, and a tasteless but filling ration bar. Her clever coat was inside its pouch, and she pulled it on gratefully.

Outside, the air was ruddy and frozen. Vole ran, slipping and falling down the mountainside, then rising and running again. When she was a handful of kilometers from the cave entrance, she powered up her taeki and called Emergency Services. The Vel.2 said□*help has been dispatched. Remain stationary.*

Not likely, Vole thought, jumping in place, to ward off the chill. Sunlight fought its way through thick clouds. Her skin glistened like wet oil on pavement, vaguely rainbow hued. The coating seemed to offer some protection. The sun disappeared, and snow began to fall.

Vole ran in place, letting herself be warmed by the light that lived in her chest, making plans. She recorded instructions into her taeki for what to do with the samples; new polymers, experimental trauma protocols, possibilities for future research. She transmitted them to herself, on Lafford, with copies sent to Xan.

Xan.□The sizzling flare reached out for him. Vole tried to form words to send, but her thoughts formed pictures instead. She put the taeki back in her bag and began catching snowflakes on her tongue.

Lights appeared through the thickly falling snow. Propellers whirred.

Two uniformed ETechs jumped down from a Terrabyl, wrapping Vole in a silver blanket and hustling her on board. The frigid air give way to sudden warmth, smells of old resin, burned tea and humans. Vole breathed it in, willing herself to come back to the living.

"How did you get all the way out here, Medic Ublion?"

"A bird dropped me," Vole said.

The Techs laughed and stopped pestering her with questions.

Chapter Sixteen

Rescued

When they had determined that she was healthy, the Techs gave Vole food, and hydration fluid. Even when her belly was full, Vole felt a sense of lightness and freedom, the giddy sensation of tossing aside a great weight. The Terrabyl was warm and smooth as they glided down the mountain slopes.

"Where are you taking me?"

"Vortex Park. Routine check, maybe they'll want some tests. It's a miracle, really. Says here you've been missing for four days," the male Tech said. He had a high bun in his black hair, and a full beard that nearly covered his face. His name tag read *Thorn*. "Where were you?"

"I crawled into a hole," Vole said, not untruthfully. "It was warm. I didn't want to risk coming out, and my taeki was frozen. Once I got it working again, I called."

"It was frozen for four days? What a piece of junk," said the female Tech, who was large and heavy, with a thick blond braid, and a name tag that read *Aanyes*. "They told us you fell into Kriki Valley. We weren't even looking for you, not with Solstice coming up. This time of year, we do routine sweeps for Daredevils trying to get some unofficial practice in."

"You thought I died?" She pictured Xan getting this news. Her light feeling ebbed away.□

"Nothing personal," Thorn smiled. "It's just, that cliff is so high, if you fall off, there's not much left to find."

Vole nodded. "I understand. Did they tell you anything about what happened to Medic Vidsonnen?"□

"He was killed in Karpolo's Reserve. They have his body." Aanyes tossed her yellow braid and punched a keyboard. "There's a replacement Medic, in from Lafford, I think. I haven't met him."

"A replacement medic from Lafford?"

"Yes, right in our busiest season. As soon as they start competing, we will have a pileup of emergencies. Hope he knows how to handle trauma."

"He does." Vole smiled. "I know him."

Thorn sounded dubious. "Really? Maybe you can explain why he's on Bilioth when his space station is under quarantine. He got in just under the wire."

"Lafford is under quarantine?"

"That's the scuttlebutt. The Authority is keeping the whole thing very quiet until after Solstice."

"They're routing traffic through a separate Command Terminus, but it's causing terrible backups, and right before the holiday." Thorn, who was monitoring the Terrabyl's auto-drive down steep pink snowbanks, turned his brown-black eyes to Vole. "I heard Lafford is being moved to the outer rim."

"That's impossible," Aanyes scoffed. "Without a Waystation, Bilioth loses most of its tourists. No way the Authority lets that happen. If something is broken up there, they'll fix it."

"What else have you heard?" Vole asked. "What other scuttlebutt?"

Thorn shrugged. "Arpina Karpolo got arrested. Something very fishy happened on the Reserve."

Aanyes said, "Rumors are flying. So far, I heard that Vidsonnen was killed by birds, snakes, Karpolo herself, a deranged Medic from Lafford..."

"That would be me," Vole said.

"Right," the woman continued. "But they also say tourists, pirates, daredevils, and angry patients. Though most people agree, he was crushed by rocks, which was an accident. Poor Grigg."

"He was a strange guy, but a great Medic," Thorn said.

"Agreed," Vole said. "But they arrested Karpolo?"

Thorn sighed. "But not for murder. I think she's charged with..."

"...Bestiality," Aanyes finished his sentence. "Or something like that."

"She's been abusing her authority for years," Thorn said. "Vidsonnen had evidence, supposedly, or he made threats. No one's sure. Something happened to her research facility."

Aanyes laughed. "The boys told me it was the birds. They attacked it."

"Good for them," Thorn said.

"You're not worried that I'm a murderer?"

Thorn smiled. "No offense, but you're pretty scrawny to pull down a rockslide."

Vole crossed her arms. "How long until we get there?"

"Why? You have some errands to run?" Thorn smiled. "We could let you out. Not that you'd get very far."

Outside the bubble, snow was giving way to boulder fields. Several large, fierce-looking marsupials stood on their haunches, watching the Terrabyl pass overhead.

"It'll be a couple of hours, hon," Aanyes said kindly. "Go ahead and get comfortable."

Vole sat back and watched out the bubble, as the landscape shifted from rocks to trees, to tundra. The next thing Vole knew, Aanyes was jostling her shoulder. "Be there soon. We're back on the Interface, if you want to exchange messages. Let your loved ones know you're okay."

Vole searched her taeki for journo pieces about Lafford, or Vidsonnen's death, but none appeared. She was able to glean only that there had been a small fire at the Good Ship Lodging, but Solstice was two days away, and they were operating as usual. The screen showed a beauty shot of the mineral pool. She had over a hundred messages, mostly from Xan, a few from Naivos. No one at the clinic had her private codes, though she could imagine many people on Lafford were trying to get hold of her, if the place was under quarantine.□

The Terrabyl hovered across the desert. To Vole's surprise, they were coming in from the South, the opposite direction from the Reserve. Red sand rippled, gray shadows snaking across it for miles. Mysterious holes opened here and there, big enough for the Terrabyl to fall into, had it been touching the ground.□

Suddenly they were at the perimeter, entering the Playplex, with its green belts and buildings, roads and pathways; a toy village, with a rusted-folly theme, peopled by stringy-haired dolls. Vole smiled at them, and one or two looked up, startled, then smiled back.□

The ring road was crowded with tourists, strung with Solstice decorations, parties spilling out of bar fronts onto the boardwalk.□ Then they were at Vortex Park Medotel's Emergency entrance. Thorn let Vole and Aanyes out, then drove off.

"Take care of yourself, Medic," the big woman smiled as she spoke. "Whatever you were up to out there, you're lucky you made it back alive. Understand?"

The Tech disappeared inside the facility.□ Vole hesitated. It felt like years since she'd exited those doors, Vidsonnen narrating pridefully. His blood still made a thin, dark rim under her fingernails.□

The automatic doors slid open. Xan stood on the other side, staring hard into Vole's face. He looked different away from the Station, taller and slenderer somehow, his dark hair cleaner than usual.□

"Medic Ublion," he said in a hard voice. "Come with me."

Chapter Seventeen

Confessions

Xan ushered Vole past reception. The human MedGens looked at her with interest, though whether they held her responsible for Vidsonnen's death, she couldn't tell.□

"Four days," he said quietly, as they entered Vidsonnen's sleek office, now markedly messier since Xan had clearly taken it over. "You left me with no information for four. Damn. Days."

"Xan."

His brown eyes were tired, and up close his stubble looked days old. He whispered: "I honestly thought you might be dead. I was...it was rough. I came down here to look for you, even though we still have cases, lots of cases..."

"Xan, I'm sorry..."

He waved her away. "...and the moment I was off-Station, Naivos closed our doors.□*Not a quarantine, just a time out,*□according to her.□*Get things under control.* She refused to send anyone looking for you. She said,□*of course the little war corpse isn't dead, but she will be when I get her in front of a disciplinary action committee.*□Apparently,□*the birds*□insisted you were fine."

"Oh, good," Vole said, trying to catch his eye. "They knew where I was."

"Oh good. The□*birds*□knew where you were."□He glared. "Which was...precisely where, on this insane dirtball?"

She stifled a smile. "Well..."

"You are not laughing at me." He stepped back.□ "Say you're not laughing at me."

She wiped her eyes. "I'm not. I'm not."□

"Vole." He pressed his eyes shut.

"I'm sorry, I just..." She laughed again, tears running down her cheeks, trying to hide her face. "I have been thinking about you, and now you're actually here, I just thought it would be different. You're just so...cute."□

"Uh huh." He regarded her coolly. "You've finally lost your actual mind, once and for all."

With great effort, Vole calmed herself. "Bilioth...does that to a person."

"Does it, now? Here and I assumed you had nothing to do with the death of Medic Vidsonnen. I've defended you, staunchly." He shook his head. "For quite a long time, actually."

"I know. If it weren't for you..." She used a sleeve to wipe her eyes. "I can explain everything. Seriously."

They stood in silence.□

Finally, he said, "Okay, then. I'll call for some tea."

She moved toward a pleasant grouping of chairs and sofas in front of a tall window. The sun filtered through trees, reminding her how carefully Vidsonnen planned every detail, how lonely he must have been. He'd been so happy for an adventure. Vole touched her heart, sending her dead friend respect.

"What is on your arm?" Xan took her wrist, pulling it into the sun. It glimmered, the hologram-like coating clearly visible in the light. "It's like..." He pulled up one of her sleeves, "...a coating of some sort. I've read about this. Where?"

Vole watched her arm in his hands, a small smile on her lips. He noticed, dropping it and stepping back. "Ooops. Sorry. I forgot. Do you...need meds now, or want to wait and see?"

She stepped toward him, taking his hand. Her breathing was steady, heart rate calm. "I don't need meds."

His eyes met hers, alarm turning to curiosity. "Who are you? And what have they done with Vole Ublion?"

Before she had time to consider the consequences, she leaned in and kissed him on the lips. His hands reached around her shoulders, pulling her in. His lips felt soft, surrounded by bristling whiskers. Her face flushed.□

They pulled back, not making eye contact.□ Vole sat on the couch, Xan on a chair.

He swallowed. "You said Bilioth□*does things to people*. What has it done to you?"

"I'll...you remember I told you I wanted to find a place where a pathogen might grow, a moist environment?"

"Of course I remember. The next morning your lodging contacted Naivos to say you'd died in a fire." He sighed. "But naturally, I refused to believe anything without a body. And then, a few hours later Naivos comes to say you'd trespassed on the Jaisenet Reserve again, and she's furious, and not only that, but the local medic here came with you and was killed in an avalanche."

"Not an avalanche, really. More like crushed by falling rocks...pierced and bled out." She felt again the rage of Vidsonnen's needless death.

"Oh." His expression changed. "Maybe you'd better tell your side of the story. The part about the birds, and you being okay."

"I came here, to this office, looking for my hoverbyl driver..." Vole did her best to explain the previous few days, hesitating at the most psychedelic parts of her Zoon odyssey.□

Xan moved in to touch her hand. "So, this is really okay?"

She smiled, stroking his face. "I think so. Though, more research is needed."

"Clearly." He looked pleased. "Let's set up an appointment. Wait...what?"

The door flew open. A pair of□soldiers wearing Authority uniforms entered, moving with ceremonial precision.□ They stepped to either side of the doorway, then backed up, standing at attention, eyes straight ahead.□

One of the soldiers said, "You will now stand for Quadrant Forum Representative Natova Naivos."

Neither Xan nor Vole moved. Naivos' heels clicked as she crossed the room. She settled her slender, tailored frame into Vidsonnen's desk chair.□"Medic Ublion. It seems you aren't dead. Account for your actions." She motioned to a seat opposite the desk.

Vole complied, sitting and regarding Naivos as if for the first time. She read great age in Naivos' fierce brown eyes. The woman had survived much of the human diaspora, then the Velraen Revolution, and after that the war. She must have lost most everyone she'd known, or loved. What was left? Desire for power, greed, or an effort to leave some kind of important legacy?□

Vole smiled. "My actions, Madame? Is this an official debrief? Last time we spoke you made it clear that I am not here as your deputy."

"You have drunk Bilioth's water, obviously." Naivos held up a manicured claw. "But that in no way excuses you from culpability."

Xan moved to the other chair, looking back and forth between the women.

"Are you accusing me of something, Madame Naivos?" Vole asked.

"I sent you here to find Oliason. That was your only job. As you are aware, I preferred to send Medic Aizmirst, but he insisted that you be the one to come."

"Thank you," Vole mouthed to Xan.□

"You failed. Not only that, you repeatedly violated Authority codes of conduct, trespassing on sanctuary ground, disturbing scientific inquiry, and worst of all, placing a valued member of the community here, a trusted Medic, in a needless position of risk which resulted in his death."

"He drove, actually," Vole said quietly. "Though I wonder if the tourist board has received the memo on not harassing the Jaisenet Birds? There was a big band of dirigible pirates shooting off rockets, with Scientist Karpolo's knowledge. Or didn't she tell you?"

"Stop talking, Medic," Naivos said. "Guards, wait outside."

The two soldiers stepped out, closing the door behind them.

"What? Something you don't want people to hear?" Xan said.

Naivos sighed. "As I said to you before, little happens in my district without my knowledge"

Xan's face clouded. "So you knew that Karpolo was allowing people to fly blimps into the Reserve."

Naivos crossed her arms. "Why would I allow something like that, Medic?"

Vole met Xan's eyes, giving him an almost imperceptible shake of the head.□

"Of course, a Forum Rep wouldn't profit from any businesses in their district, isn't that right?"

"There are strict regulations, of course," Naivos said. "But profit is allowed, in some instances."

"Only if the business at hand is legal."

"Correct." Naivos looked pleased with herself.

"And shooting off rockets to scare giant birds into flight, for the enjoyment of tourists, would not be?"

"Also correct," Naivos said. "So you see why I could have had nothing to do with it. Though if Arpina did, she'll have to face the consequences."

"I see," Vole said, remembering how enraged the old woman had been. "And, a business partnership with Oliason, that would be perfectly acceptable?"

Naivos shrugged. "Of course. Forum Reps have rights, as citizens of the diaspora, to reasonable sources of income. Same as anyone else."

Xan's eyes flitted back and forth between Vole and Naivos, a look of comprehension dawning. "Oliason was your business partner."□

"Was? Is. I had hoped to discover his whereabouts. But your partner here," she gestured dismissively toward Vole, "has spent her entire time on-planet goofing off, spending money, and having a high old time. Not delivering Oli to me, as instructed. Not sealing off his putrid infection, sad to say."

Vole giggled.□

"Oh, you find this amusing," Naivos said sarcastically. "I hope that when you're in the brig, serving time, on my recommendation, you'll have a good long laugh."

"When I'm in the brig?" Vole said, brow furrowing.□"For not delivering you your business partner?"

"Is that some kind of threat?" Naivos crossed her legs, leaning back in the chair. She smiled a faint smile. She was enjoying herself.

Xan sat forward. "Madame Naivos. Who is caring for the patients on Lafford Waystation?"

"Now that you've reunited with Medic Ublion, you are free to return to Lafford. But only you. The pathogen must be kept sealed. We can't expect innocent travelers to be exposed to danger."

Vole stifled a giggle at the thought of people on Bilioth avoiding danger, when so many of them deliberately sought it out.

Xan's face reddened. "You know people will die because of your actions."

Naivos patted her hair absently. "True. That's how sickness works, Medic. But I am in a position to decide which sort of people. And I choose those who are already in a diseased environment, not those who simply want to visit Bilioth for a bit of pleasure."

Vole made her chair swivel back and forth. "Important that word not get out though. Might put a damper on the celebrations. Eh? Hurt business?"

Naivos met her eyes. "Where is Oliason? What is he sitting on, that sly devil? Hm? You're not a stupid girl, war corpse though you may be, scrubbed and wiped on Authority's dime. You're a good diagnostician. What did you find out?"

"Don't talk to her that way," Xan said in a flustered voice.

"It's okay." Vole made a calming motion. "It's all true. I'll tell you. But no more threats, Madame."

"Or what?" Naivos rolled her eyes. "You're going to bring me up on charges of doing my utmost to protect a planet, in my district? Go ahead."

"I might, for example, petition the Forum for a list of people you own insurance policies for. See if Oliason is on it."

Naivos laughed, clutching at the heavy silver chain at her throat, "You'd never have access to that. No one would, it's highly restricted."

"Yes, data is restricted. And yet, Karpolo knows so much."

After a beat, Naivos replied: "Arpina is old. She's been around long enough to compile her own data. Though," she made a sad face, "I believe all her records were destroyed recently. So we'll never know."

"Mmmm," Vole said. "You're going to have me arrested for trespassing and shut me away, and, what, have Lafford Station moved to the Outer Rim, so the tourist trade on Bilioth isn't hurt when the truth comes out about the outbreak?"

Naivos shrugged. "My job is to solve problems. But you're underestimating my interest in Oli."

"Am I?" Vole asked.□

"He's worth far more to me than his insurance policy, though that's not meager. No, Oli is more than an employee, more than a cunning ship commander, good with negotiations, always finding new markets, new products... Oli has a genius for seeking out that certain something..." She leaned forward, eyes gleaming, "That wild experience that gives human beings an alive feeling."

"That they are willing to pay for," Vole agreed.

"Oh, happy to pay for," Naivos continued. "I know that you have some idea what Oli's next venture was going to be. And I know that you will tell me everything the birds told you."

Vole pictured the Zoons. She patted the side of her bag, with the samples of their water. Medicine, not a wild experience, though it was that, too. She thought about Oli's cold body, adrift in the lake, deliberately silent.□

"Madame, I know you're joking about speaking to birds," Vole said. "And honestly, I haven't had any communications with Oliason."

Naivos pushed her chair away from the desk, rising and calling the soldiers in from the hallway.□

"Place this woman in under arrest, for trespassing on protected land, insubordination, and...let's see...dereliction of duty." She winked and walked out the door.◻

Against Xan's protests, the two Authority soldiers moved toward Vole.

Chapter Eighteen

The Leona

"Medic, this woman is under arrest." The two guards pushed Xan away.

He pushed back, uselessly. "This is insane. What are you doing?"

"Don't, Xan."

"We are in the middle of an epidemic!" He shouted. "This woman is a Medic."

The guards ignored him. One held Vole, while the other took out a pair of hand restraints.

"Don't put those on her. She hates..." His voice trailed off as one of the guards shoved him halfway across the room.

Vole said calmly, "I'll be fine. These charges are a smoke screen."

"Ma'am, I suggest you keep your thoughts to yourself. Madame Naivos is very good at getting convictions. Anything you say can be used against you," said the taller of the young, dark-haired guards. They looked enough alike that it was clear they came from the same tribe, if not the same family.

"Thank you," Vole said, holding out her wrists.

"Hey, idiots," came a voice from the doorway.

Minna, looking healthier than Vole had ever seen her, wore oversize men's clothing so fine it could only have come from raiding Vidsonnen's closet. Her Mohawk stood on end, covered in red glitter over the red dye, like a truly fabulous war helmet.□

"Your boss is getting accosted in the entryway," she said to the guards. "Someone screaming about taxes? There's a whole gang of them. Old Lady Naivos already broke three nails."

The two men exchanged a look.

Minna continued, in a bossy tone, "The Medotel only has Gens for security, and they're unarmed. She's getting□roughed up! Have you never been on-surface before? Planets are dangerous!"

"Stay here, Ma'am," the tall guard said. "Evading federal arrest is worse than what you're charged with. Don't run." He and his partner hurried down the hall.

Vole smiled, and Minna came in for a hug, squealing. "They said you fell off the Kriki Cliff. Why would they say something□like that? So specifically deadly? And here you are. Looking...so sparkly."

Vole laughed. "Naivos isn't being mugged, is she?"

"Of course not. Hi Medic Aizmirst." Minna darted to Vidsonnen's desk and began rummaging around in it. After a moment, she smiled triumphantly, holding up a key fob.□ "It's only going to take them a second to figure out I lied. Follow me."□

Alarms sounded as the three piled down a back staircase and out onto the ground floor.□ They passed three Vel.2s and a human Med-Gen in blue scrubs, who smiled and held open a door as they scurried out into an alley. No one seemed to want them to stop, or even slow down.

"This way. Help me," Minna said. Vidsonnen's black Leona sat under a cover, which they unzipped and whipped off. "This Leona was

Grigg's baby. When they towed it in, I knew something terrible had happened."

She jumped into the driver's seat. Vole followed. Xan hesitated. "As soon as I get in, I'm a criminal."

"Too late for that," Vole said. "The moment you stopped being part of Naivos' plans, your future was forfeit."

"But, I haven't done anything." His eyes pleaded. "You really think she'd ruin someone's life just so she could get away with bending the rules for profit?"

The women stared.

"Yeah, you're right." He jumped in. Before he'd even hit the seat, Minna gunned it out of the alley. She took side streets onto the ring road, heading west to the Oligidisi District. They passed the Aviary, which was dark, its front windows boarded up.□

"What happened?"

Minna smiled, "Rumor has it, somehow all the glass got smashed."

"Hmm," Vole said. "Now why would anyone do a thing like that?"

"Thanks for making sure I got taken care of after the accident, by the way. You and Aizmirst are good Medics. He cured my...problem."

"I'm sorry I didn't realize you had it. You didn't mention the rash, or any of the other symptoms."

Minna shrugged, spinning the Leona past a group of Komis. "I didn't know you were a Medic. Madame Naivos told a friend of mine that a lady named Vole Ublion was coming down to meet with Oli. She wanted you followed, but not by anyone in her organization who might be loyal to Oli. She approached my friend, who knew I was looking for Oli anyway. So I volunteered. It never occurred to me that she would send you all the way down here without knowing where he was. She must have been really desperate."

"She was," Vole said. "I thought I was chasing the source of the epidemic. In reality, Naivos was just trying to make sure her business partner wasn't crossing her. She figured, if no one on-planet was willing to give him up to her, maybe I'd convince them it was for the greater good."

The storefronts of Oligidisi passed, windows gleaming fuschia in the low sun.□Naivos had been right, Vole thought. Oli was crossing her. But just not in the way she expected. In the end, Oliason had chosen to die with the greatest discovery of all, the powerful magic of the Ertsu Zoons□ as his secret. And now that secret was Vole's. She felt the glow in her chest, the connection she had with them, and would always have.

The Kolmi riders, a dozen or more in shiny, skin-tight uniforms with corporate logos, waved in admiration as the byl hovered over them. Some hooted gleefully.□

"That stuff just never occurred to me. I figured you were someone Oli owed money to, or he had flirted with you, and by flirting I mean hooked up with and then ditched, or maybe he was being investigated by some Authority agency. Most likely the last one, no offense. But your clothes..." Minna made an apologetic face.

Vole laughed. "None taken."

"This Oliason sounds like a complete scoundrel," Xan said from the back seat.

"No." "No." The two women said simultaneously.

Minna brought them back to a normal hover a meter off the ground. The business district was giving way to residential and park land. They took a right turn onto a wide street. On either side, star ships lay parked amidst landscaped yards, some with vegetable gardens or poultry coops. Children ran, laughing, and goats cropped grass.

"Oli got caught up□building the Playplex into a destination resort. He thought it would do people a world of good to come here, especially anyone who had been in the war and needed a mood lifter. He was very into love and joy, and he thought business was a necessary part of all that. Which is true. I was furious with him for getting me sick. But now, I just hope he gets help."

"I don't think that's going to happen, Minna," Vole said softly. "I'm sorry."

The two women exchanged a look.□Outside, white-blossomed trees flanked a wide beer garden full of revelers at long tables. The sun was low. Music from a live band advanced and receded as they passed.

"Did you get to know Oliason?" Xan asked Vole.□

"In a way," Vole said. "I think he found a limit to what he was willing to do, for the sake of humans. I think...he wanted to keep us from taking too much advantage of other species. And he was willing to sacrifice for that."

Minna's eyes filled with tears. "That's good to know."

"Where are we going?" Xan asked Minna.□ He turned to Vole. "And why aren't you more worried?"□

"We're invited for cocktails," Minna said.□

Chapter Nineteen

Nyppio

Minna turned into a long, unkempt, gravel drive flanked by large trees strewn with lacy lichen reminiscent of camo.

"Cocktails?" Xan said. "With whom?"

"A friend of your partner's," Minna laughed. "Who wants to□*fix the mess*. At least he said he did."

The Leona pulled up to a star ship that lay half-buried in vegetation. It was a common model from twenty years previous, a□*Sparks Minnow*, Vole recalled. Visible below the vines, the ship's fuselage had been airbrushed with pin-up girls, sitting atop various planets and smiling out lasciviously.

"A friend...of yours?" Xan looked at Vole.

"A freinemy, really. If it's who I think it is."□

Minna brought the byl to stop, and they all jumped out. A tall, white-braided man emerged from the air lock.□

"Nyppio," Vole said.

"Get inside, quickly please." The older man's eyes crinkled into a tense half-smile. "They still have satellites."

"The Authority is spying? In spite of the Armistice Declaration?" Xan sounded disappointed, but not shocked.

Nyppio pulled them onto the ship. "No doubt they would say it's the price we pay for peace. Whatever you call it, no one around here intends to cooperate. Not only are we patriots, but we like our freedom. Miss, you have more support than you think."

"I do?" Vole asked, as they passed inside. "What do you mean?"

"Please," Nyppio led them deeper into the ship, which felt surprisingly space-worthy, introducing a handful of crew members, who had the air of a team busily preparing for something. Two of them, young men named Quaid and Dagg, looked familiar to Vole. They seemed different than they had at the Good Ship; still physically impressive, but with a friendly, relaxed demeanor that gave a strong impression that the two weren't always ripping apart robots, and setting fire to buildings.

Minna pushed past. "Nypps. I'm starving. Got anything to eat?"

"I was about to offer refreshments, as per inter-galactic custom. Do you think me a barbarian? Child, don't touch anything," Nyppio glared. "Or anyone."

"I'm not contagious," Minna smiled. "Medic Aizmirst cured me."

"Good." Nyppio said with a look of genuine relief. He turned to Vole: "Apologies for...what happened at the Good Ship. As I said, nothing personal."□

Xan moved closer. "You had something to do with the fire?"

Nyppio looked contrite. "Unfortunately, yes. Though, I made sure Miss herself was safe at all times."

"That in no way comforts me," Xan glared.

"Please," Nyppio motioned for them to enter a room that had the look of the inside of a particularly modern cave. "I'm the ranking member of the Freighters Guild for this quadrant. All of the guilds have a close relationship with Oli, but the Freighters work for him directly. When I met Miss, she appeared to be colluding with Madam Naivos to harm the Commander in some way."

"And when I stayed at such an expensive lodging, that didn't exactly make me look like an ordinary citizen."□

"I can't say it helped, no. Not to be critical, but your hair, your clothes, your lack of jewels of any kind," Nyppio said.

"You looked poor and backward, Medic," Minna called out. "No offense. You seem a lot better now."

"Staying at the Good Ship made me seem...like an accomplice of some sort. If not for Naivos, then for someone with means, am I right?"

"Yes, and as I said in the bar that night, not someone who was paying you for sex," Nyppio said.

Xan's eyes flashed. "Have either of□*you*□two looked in a mirror lately?"

□Vole made a calming gesture, then took a seat on an upholstered couch near Nyppio. "You knew Naivos was corrupt?"

"We've known for a long time. She's been part of this place since the beginning. But Oli was always there to smooth things over, make sure our business was protected from her control. She has been after us to do her bidding, none of which is strictly legal. Without Oli to keep her happy, Naivos can de-legitimize the Freighters any time she wants. You know, portray us as thugs, tie us up in litigation and replace us with her own people. She has information."

"And anything she doesn't have, she'll invent," Xan said.

"I see you've met her," Nyppio sighed. "Not someone who takes no for an answer."

Vole crossed her arms. "I noticed Scientist Karpolo knew quite a bit about me. That was when I began to wonder. Is she also under Naivos' thumb? How deep does this go?"□

"Believe me, Naivos has something on everyone. Oli said she must have been collecting for years. Possibly, since before the war. I mean, who really knows what parts of the grid were left operational?" Nyppio looked up toward the ceiling, as if watching for satellites. "Oli had this idea—to confront her about her hoard. He wanted to do it in public, on the floor of the Forum, with as many other reps and witnesses as he could. It seemed like a good plan. He's the original AUD Champion, famous throughout the diaspora. There'd be Journos interested."— His amber eyes clouded. "Obviously, he never made it."

"Nypps, you know he got the baddest rash anyone's ever had," Minna called out. "But being Oli, he ignored it."

"Wait," Xan asked, "Oliason's infection flared just as he took it upon himself to make a trip to Forum Station?"

"Apparently," Nyppio shrugged. "Convenient coincidence."

"You think that witch invented the damned rash, just to silence Oli?" Minna asked. "Woah."

Xan leaned back on the couch. "That's pretty farfetched, scientifically."

Vole picked at a piece of webbing at the hem of her tunic, watching her holographic skin gleam in the ship's lights. "Naivos couldn't have been using Sairasma to manipulate Oliason. When I saw him, he was in the end stages, too sick to be cured, even if we had the polymer then."—

"I blame her anyway," said Minna. "I just like blaming her."

"Do you think he knew how far gone he was?" Xan asked.

"I do." Vole's mind replayed her interactions with Oliason in the clinic. "As soon as I told him I had never seen his rash before, and I'd need time to figure out what it was...he ran." She didn't voice her next thought,—*he had something more important to take care of on Bilioth, than trying to save his own life.*

"It just doesn't make sense," Xan said. "He must have been in unbearable pain. Even palliative care would have benefited him."

"I think Oliason stumbled into a... moral dilemma." Vole didn't want to explain that the Zoons were alchemists. She believed that in their magical way, they invented the virus, not to kill but to ward people off. She imagined Oliason working with them to find a way to end interest in the protected areas of Bilioth. A virus, spread around enough to scare the public, connected in some mysterious way to the Pleasure Planet "I asked aggressively where he'd picked up the infection. I'm sure I sounded truly determined to find the source. And Naivos was on-station then, remember? Now we know why. She was going to confront Oliason before he ever got to Forum Station."

"That's a moral dilemma?" Xan asked. "Then he blew it. He could have infected Her Highness and brought his karma load down to zero."

Nyppio and Minna agreed.

Vole touched her heart absently, remembering the loving presence of the giant worms, the white fire that burned invisibly in her chest. Vole didn't think the Zoons would intentionally sicken her. But she was immunized, so she'd never know. What else could creatures with only chemistry as a weapon do to defend themselves? She imagined Oliason's pain being eased in their water, dying with a clear conscience, believing they would live on undisturbed. It made Vole feel close to him, the one other person on Bilioth who had experienced their magic.

"This explains why Naivos sent Oli's ship the Rausku to the Hevoxin Corridor," Nyppio said. "She said it was to retrieve more hardware. She was trying to force him to build more infrastructure on Bilioth. Make it look like Oli was the greedy one." Nyppio sounded disgusted. "He couldn't take it. It wasn't what he stood for, at all."

"Oh, yeah!" Minna said. "With the Rausku out of system, harder for Oli to sneak off to Forum Station."

"Okay, but why would a revered scientist like Arpina Karpolo co-operate with Naivos?" Xan asked. "Karpolo had the law on her side. A stellar reputation, a famous dead Daredevil for a son. What does Naivos have over her?"

"You said it. Sharm," Vole said quietly. She thought about the way the old woman's eyes had softened when she talked about him.□

"The damn fool kid. Sweet, everyone liked him. But dumb as rocks," Nyppio said. "He died trying to win his second AUD prize. Very sad."

"Not everyone liked him. My girlfriend Mindallia said he was afraid to even talk to a girl, or a boy, either. So shy he could only be around animals, she said. I never met him, myself," Minna said.

"Vidsonnen was Sharm Karpolo's Medic." Vole slipped off her shoes and put them under her. "He told me the kid died over Kriki-Valley, because the birds didn't catch him when he fell."

"Harsh way to go," Minna said. "Kind of pure, but still."

"That's awful," Xan said.□

"Arpina was mean as hell to him when he was alive," Nyppio observed quietly. "But they didn't deserve that."

"Come on, Nypps. It's classic." Minna spun in slow circles. "Sharm died because those birds his mother loves so much refused to save his ass. And Naivos was planning to tell the world, if the old lady didn't pimp them out."

"Karpolo must have come to hate the Jaisenets." Vole rubbed her eyes. "Poor woman. She was so proud of that ugly trophy."

"Didn't you say that those same birds carried you to the..." Xan searched for the right word, "mountains?"

"Yes," Vole nodded. "For whatever reason, they chose to save me."

"What's this?" Nyppio asked. "So, you actually did fall off Kriki Cliff?"

"Yes. I think the Jaisenets are on our side, Nyppio. But even more so. I think they want all humans off Bilioth."

"Amen," said Minna. "I would."

A beautiful, gray-haired woman in a floral tunic entered, setting out a tray of colorful drinks, fruit and sandwiches. Nyppio introduced her as Lestia. "She's actually our navigator. I try to stay away from Velraens on my crew. They're efficient, but they make such unimaginative cocktails."

Lestia smiled. "Let me know if you need anything more, Nypps. Welcome aboard, everyone."

She disappeared down a passageway.

Nyppio passed around drinks. "A toast to Oli."

Each of them raised a glass. Vole had selected a tumbler with amber liquid garnished with what looked like green citrus peel, though it might have been a caterpillar. She didn't want to look too closely. The drink tasted smoky, sweet, and strong, and she intended to finish it.□

When they had toasted, Vole reached into her bag and pulled out the head lamp, handing it to Nyppio.

"I can tell you for a certainty that Oliason has moved on to a better place. I'm convinced it was where he wanted to be."□

Nyppio turned the lamp over in his□hands,□lips a tight line. "Guess he wanted to die with dignity?"

"I think it was more than that," Vole said.□

"So weird to think of Oli being dead." Minna lowered a sandwich from her mouth, mid-bite. "Were you there?"

Xan said, "He was already gone when you found him, you said."

"He was," Vole said, meeting Nyppio's amber eyes. "I believe he wanted the source of the infection to be safely sealed off. He had his reasons. And they were noble. I think more than anything, Oliason wanted to make sure that no other species would be abused, the way the birds are. He..." She thought about the Zoons. "My hunch is, he truly loved this planet, and he didn't want to participate in exploiting it anymore. He thought I'd never find him, never find the source. And I wouldn't have. The one variable he missed was the birds. They knew exactly where he was."

"So they took *you* to him?" Nyppio asked. "Why you?"

"I can't be sure." She didn't want to talk about the cavern, or what she had experienced there. "But the airships that killed Vidsonnen must not have been the first to show up and harass the birds. Not if Karpolo's rage is any indication. That cliff side is the Jaisenet's nesting ground, the place they raise their chicks. If Naivos was forcing Karpolo to allow tourists to shoot off cannons on top of performing in the Aviary, the birds would understand she was no longer capable of protecting them. They also knew that I had gotten thrown out of the Aviary for pitching a fit. Maybe they decided I was worth a shot."

"You got thrown out of the Aviary? For pitching a fit?" Minna asked, laughing. "You're my new hero."

Nyppio stood and offered everyone another round. "So, Oli is not going to show up and lead us into a minor rebellion against our corrupt Quadrant Forum Rep."

"And we can't go back to Lafford, until we clear Vole's name," Xan said.

"The only way out of this is to beat Naivos at her own game." Nyppio sipped his whiskey. "You were right about me, by the way. This is the finest sour mash this side of Obbney."

Xan looked back and forth between the two. "You've only been down here for a week."

"I also read you as a decent man," Vole said. "So tell me this, Nyppio. Who rents out those absurd, tricked-out, fully armed airships?"

The older man broke out in a sunny smile, and Minna started to laugh. Xan didn't say anything, but the look on his face was dubious.

Chapter Twenty

Sparks Rise

Within minutes, Nyppio's ship, the *Nola Belle*, was speeding out of the Playplex, heading south. Black desert passed below them, sky above deep burgundy. When they had put some distance between themselves and the Playplex, Nyppio rejoined his guests.

"I can't stop thinking about Earth," Vole said. "When I should be trying to get back to Lafford."

Only Xan knew about the vials of water in her bag, the Zoon blood, and Oliason's. They needed a lab. And to get one, Vole thought to herself with a sigh, there was no alternative to somehow exposing, disabling, or blackmailing Natova Naivos. But even amid that daunting reality, Vole kept falling into a loopy, dream-like feeling. Earth appeared in her imagination, the beautiful blue pearl refusing to be pushed away from the center of her thoughts.

"Earth?" Xan made a puzzled face. "I can't tell if this adventure has helped you, or if it's thrown you over the edge."

He was sitting next to her, holding her hand, passing it back and forth between his own as if she'd float away without him. Vole liked it.

Minna had fallen asleep in the swing chair. Nyppio and Lestia moved in and out, setting up a large dinner table, introducing other crew members, and filling in gaps in the story that was now spreading through the Playplex; Madame Naivos would be taking part in the Solstice Parade, which was notoriously raucous, in a transparent ploy for popularity in her district. Elections weren't for two standard years, but something had made her call around, looking for staff, and a suitable vehicle.

"Like I said," Nyppio said as he sat near Vole and Xan, "People talk to me. No one likes Naivos. And I hope you don't mind, but I let fly that Oli died. I didn't specifically implicate her, but the timing is clear enough."

Vole considered. "If Naivos finds out..."

"She's no doubt finding out as we speak. Bilioth is..."

"...Vidsonnen told me. A small place. Won't Naivos use that knowledge to implicate me somehow?"

"She's already implicated you, hasn't she?" Nyppio said. "Anyone who's paying attention will notice, Naivos is trying to take down anyone in her path. People here loved Oli. They won't take kindly to the notion that you were looking to cure him, which you can easily prove, since not only did you get thrown out of the Aviary in front of witnesses, but you also had your fire in the Good Ship, and she's put out a warrant for your arrest. It all makes Naivos look like she's trying to frame you."

Xan shrugged. "It's good you got noticed by so many locals. We have records on Lafford that could clear you, but huh. Can't access them now."

"She's going to make sure I disappear, one way or another. Nyppio, can I speak to Lastia? She's a physicist? I have questions about Earth."

"Did you notice she's Earthen?" The older man stared at her thoughtfully. "I am too, for that matter."

"I didn't know, but that's helpful," Vole said. "I realize all of this is classified. But how is Earth now? What is the Velraen infestation? How much focused energy would the human race need to take back our home planet?"

"Take back Earth?" Xan gasped, grabbing both her hands. "You have had a very long day."

Nyppio broke eye contact. "Lastia and I are both pretty well-informed about Earth in spite of the news blackouts, and we still have access to the Libraries on Forum Station, so...it will take research but...we can dream on it."

Vole watched the horizon shift from a straight line to a bumpier one. "Naivos said something to me about her constituents. She said they are happy to pay for experiences that make them feel alive. And Oliason, for all his wrong-headedness, sacrificed so that humans could get a sense of...excitement, or meaning, whatever you want to call it. He didn't know how badly people would need the Playplex. Isn't that right?"

"No one did. For years, this place was an obscure backwater. We liked it that way," Nyppio said.

"What's that got to do with Earth?" Xan asked. "And why are we not ascending?"

Nyppio cleaned his teeth with his tongue, then said, "If we leave surface, they'll see. But on planet, in the dark, it will take her longer to track us."

"Oh." Xan shifted Vole's fingers from one hand to the other, "Is it safe to use my taeki?"

"We're off the interface. But Lafford is still closed, if that's what you're concerned about. The Journos report that a team of Gens was ordered in from Command, because the regular Medics flew the coop, and our Forum Rep had to step in and save the day. Looks like your patients are reasonably well taken care of, even if not by you." Nyppio's eyes crinkled.

Xan's lips curled ever so slightly. "Command Gens are usually pretty good, though they're not trained to iterate new polymers..."

"It'll be okay." Vole squeezed his fingers. "You and I created a good protocol. If these substitute Gens follow it, people will get treated. If they don't, we still have to stop Naivos."

"Sure." Xan sighed. "How?"

"Earth," Vole said.

The men stared at her.

She smiled as the idea formed. "Earth. Instead of Bilioth."

Xan burst out laughing. It woke Minna, who sat up, rubbing her eyes. "God, I thought you people hated loud noises. Hey, is that...dinner?"

"In a minute, Child." Nyppio sat back and crossed his legs. "Earth instead of Bilioth?"

"Vidsonnen told me about the kind of people who come here. It's mostly those who are too young to remember the war. But they grew up during wartime."

"Yeah, we did." Minna moved closer, grabbing a roll from the dinner table. "It's all we've ever heard about."

"Right," Vole continued. "All these kids on Bilioth, they come for that alive feeling."

"Or for that party feeling," Minna said. "Whichever comes first."

"But the Daredevils? What is the point of adventure contests? If not to prove yourself, do rare and exciting things?"

"Yeah, you're not wrong," Minna agreed, throwing a leg over the arm of a couch. "That and to be famous."

"If you can't be a war hero, be a champion on Bilioth," Xan said.

"Move all that to a real war zone?" Nyppio said. "Ambitious plan."

"War? Really?" Xan scowled.

"Maybe not," Vole said. "But a project that requires serious sacrifice. One that's got some meaning."

"But, Vel.1s?" Xan said.

Nyppio smiled, "If they don't have star ships, they can't fight a war."

"How many Vel.1s are there, really? Does anyone know?"

"Command does, no doubt. I'm sure Madame Naivos does."

"Well, there you go," Xan said sarcastically. "Just find a way to monetize Earth."

"Right?" Minna said. "And grow some good dope there. People will come."

Nyppio's face changed. "It's the birthplace of our whole species. We've milked the planet for all it was worth, over millennia. Much as I'd dearly love to go home...is it fair to Earth?"

"There are only a handful of millions of humans left," Xan said. "No matter what planet we're on, it's going to take a thousand generations to regrow our numbers. A place like this, with a fragile ecosystem, can be destroyed by only a few thousand people. But Earth...we're already a part of that ecosystem."

"You could even argue, that it's the only place we have any right to live," Vole said.

"Look you guys." Minna pointed out the window, where they had slowed. "Harkness Canyon."

Around them, sparks rose, tiny stars or more likely insects, minute specks of light moving upward like smoke. The Nola Belle plunged down steeply but some mechanism Vole hadn't experienced before allowed the lounge to rotate comfortably in spite of the ship's angle.

"I know that the Authority agreed to terms that took Earth off the table," Vole said. "But I think it's time to renegotiate."

Xan laughed. "How in the hell?"

"I now pronounce you an honorary member of the Freighters local 90899." Nyppio made a gesture in the air. "Due to your excellent way of thinking."

"You want to declare war on Earth?" Minna took a swig from a wine glass. "Aren't there like, a million angry robots there?"

"Are they angry, though?" Vole asked. "Has anyone ever asked exactly what the Vel.1s want?"

The three gazed at her. She thought about the machine men she'd gunned down, the way their red eyes had winked out below the water. "How much of a sense of purpose can the Velraens have, without humans?"

"Apparently, enough to murder millions of us," Xan said. "I think you were there. You know this."

"I know that they can be killed. They have no more right to our home than we do. And I believe that millions of humans would be willing to do their part, to have a home. Not only would they, I believe they need to. All this Daredevilry, all these crazy creative projects. Don't you see? The only difference between that and something real is that here, we're guests. On Earth, we'd be doing something honest."□

"You're turning into a goddess, Miss." Minna smiled lazily. "I don't think Naivos knows what she's gotten herself into."

"Bilioth is going to take itself back. Just, trust me on this."

No one contradicted her. Outside, the sparks had given way to a velvet blackness darker than any she'd seen in space.

"Agreed that we need to ease up on tourism on this planet. But Earth?" Nyppio said.

Vole stood and walked to the table. Lestia and the other crew members began to steam in, carrying bowls of steaming food.

"We're at bottom, Skipper," Quaid said, smiling slyly at Minna. "Should we invite our guests to the table? It's Solstice Eve, you know."

Minna jumped up and moved toward the feast.

"What about the airships?" Xan asked. "I thought we were going after the pirates or whatever they were...?"

"Tomorrow," Nyppio replied. "We're not going after them. We're teaming up with them."

"The food smells amazing," Minna said. "Good thing I spent the last week not eating."

"Come to the table, friends," Lastia called out. "I heard Medic Ublion say something about taking back Earth from the Velraens. I want to talk about that."

The four men who had attacked the Good Ship, including Quaid and Dag, and five other, older crew members, moved to sit around the table.

"Please," Nyppio motioned for Xan and Vole to take places. "We have a short-term objective, which is to straighten things out with Madame Naivos. Let's have us a good family discussion about this long-term scheme of yours."

At that moment, each person at the table began talking at once, enthusiastically, over one another until the lounge was full of voices. Vole laughed so hard that she had to dry her eyes with her napkin.

Only Xan sat in silence, watching Vole, a look she'd never seen before spreading across his face, as if he was seeing her clearly for the very first time.

Chapter Twenty-One

Solstice

At duskwind the next evening, Vole and Xan sat in a pair of folding chairs, under a tree in Vortex Park. They had a clear view of the parade route from atop a small knoll. Everywhere, people gathered in groups with lighted objects in playful shapes. The air was full of drumming, and distant horns from someone's homespun orchestra. Xan hadn't let go of Vole's hand since they left the Nola Belle.

"This planet just feels like an accident waiting to happen. Just look at those morons." He indicated a field, where manned kites were rising off the grass, like a school of neon manta rays against the garnet dusk. Men and women hung from bars on their underside, tiny and fragile as dolls.

"Hey, we're on a mission here. Try to look like you're enjoying yourself."

"Are you kidding?" He put his face next to hers. "This is the most fun I've had in years."

"Oh yeah? What part?"

"You, of course." His teeth gleamed in the low light. "The miraculous transformation of Vole Ublion."

"Kaaki Kurtsonni", She said. It felt good to hear her birth name spoken. Satisfying, somehow, like the smell of long-forgotten perfume.

"There's a chance everything that happened to you in that cavern was a hallucination, you know that, right?" He looked apologetic.□

"Of course." She smiled, to show she wasn't offended. "What do you think. Medic? Do you think the Zoons implanted me with false memories?"

"I don't think you'd be so...happy" He waved his hands around her in a worshipful gesture. "Brain control doesn't actually free people, it just attaches their conscious mind to a false narrative. Whatever those creatures did, it feels...genuine."

She sighed. "Does it matter?"

He looked at her sidelong. "Ah, you mean, as long as the patient is cured, don't ask too many questions?"

Vole smiled. "It's a gift."

Xan kissed her, then returned his attention to the sky. "The best damn gift I've ever received."

The previous night on the Nola Belle had been alternately intense, because neither one of them wanted to stop testing to see how far her new tolerance for touching would go, and silly, because her body announced its boundaries by becoming extremely ticklish. More than once, they had to halt a passionate moment because Vole had burst out in uncontrollable giggles. It was early morning before they'd slept.

In the morning, the Nola Belle had moved again, this time to a landscape of massive volcanoes. To Vole's amazement, not far from a field of molten orange lava lay a series of enormous hangars, where a crew of thirty or so pirates ran tours in tattooed white dirigibles, like the ones in the Preserve when Vidsonnen had died. She couldn't tell which of the myriad protrusions on every part of the ships' gondolas were working armaments, and which merely cool looking accessories. Ordinance was piled everywhere, indicating that most of the guns were not just decorative.

The Pirate Captain, a red-bearded man named Deuce, offered to help before they even asked.□ His freckled face flushed with anger. "Some stupid journo write-up came out, telling people that a Jaisenet swarm was a major bucket-lister. Said to rent from us or one of our competitors, had instructions on what to do to make the birds fly, and everything."

Nyppio and Vole exchanged a look. "A journo?"

"Yeah, out of Forum Station, of course. Promoting Bilioth, you know, as a place where there are no rules." Deuce looked disgusted. "Whatever you need to shut that crap down, we're in."

Vole and Xan took a slow ride back to the Playplex in Deuce's Zeppelin. The air around the perimeter was filled with flying machines, so varied and unlikely looking that the two Medics could only stand on the observation deck, gaping.

The Zeppelin set down in the restricted part of the space port. Vole couldn't say exactly what was so sinister about the place, except that it was full of weird spacecraft, most with outbuildings and makeshift gazebos, and muscular dogs padding around with sentry-like airs.□ Motoblys were lined up in preparation for the Solstice parade, and while their riders had on tough looking jackets and studded pants, Vole didn't find them the least bit frightening.□The place reminded her of a trailer park in an old cine, part junkyard, part small town. She liked it.

Two Pirates had dropped Vole and Xan in Vortex Park, handing them a sack full of the chits everyone used as money. The plan was for them to hide in plain sight. The Pirates had supplied them with tunics, and face paint, and Minna dressed Vole's hair in a complicated undo. Even their Gens on Lafford wouldn't have recognized the two Medics. They bought food and drink and folding chairs, then set up to wait.□

Already, Solstice Fest fires were burning, and people were twirling, either stoned or happy or both. Vole laughed as Xan's eyes tracked people around them, concern growing on his face.

"You're clocked out, Medic," she said.

He gave an embarrassed smile. "This just looks like one medical emergency after another waiting to happen."

"Yup," she agreed. "You want to go volunteer? It would probably take Naivos at least half an hour to have you arrested."

He sighed, muttering. "*Bucket list item*. I'll show her a bucket list item."

At duskwind, crowds lined up on either side of the ring road, the deep rose sky filling with lights and contraptions, and an ecstatic thrum of trance music. The area over the central lake exploded into fireworks, and the parade began.□□

Vole put her hands over her mouth to keep people from seeing how hard she was laughing, watching Xan's face as he reacted to each new wave of colorful participants.□ The crowd called out their appreciation, buzzed kazoos, and clapped. Fingers of light on long sticks waved around a team of gymnasts, who flipped and pranced. A group of drummers in animal head masks and glowing jewelry followed, their beats reverberating through Vole's chest. Floats passed in slow procession, in shapes of animals, people, or elaborate geometries. Riders, representing the Guilds and major tour companies smiled and waved. Burlesque performers rolled themselves up in dangling silk sashes. The most prominent adventure outfitter offered a huge, hovering bubble, laughing children zipping around it in jet packs.

Xan's face, lit by orange strobes, looked puzzled.□ "This is awesome. But...why all this effort for something so utterly ephemeral? It seems like a waste."□□

Vole considered. "Isn't it kind of the same as what you and I do every day at the clinic?"

"What?" He looked flummoxed.□

"Healing people gives our lives purpose. Obviously, everyone we save will eventually die. But we treat them anyway."

He stared, the orange reflections on his cheeks changing to blue. "What we do is Science. This here is...entertainment"

"One person's art form is another person's magic elixir. You can't say one path is inherently better than all the others.□ If I've learned one thing in the last week, it's that."

"I don't know. But I'm glad you're so open minded." Xan's face lit up in a turquoise-tinted grin. "Tell me this new you isn't going to wear off."

"Nothing is permanent, but I do believe my woo-woo is here to stay." Vole grabbed his arm. "Go time."

The next float was a massive white-neon throne covered in sparklers and patriotic pennants. Naivos sat in the place of honor, eyes hidden behind huge glasses, gloved hand waving absently as she looked down upon the crowd. Her perch was flanked by four armored guards. Voices died as the Quadrant Rep passed. A loudspeaker blared her voice reading the Armistice Declaration.

"Where's Deuce?" Xan scanned the sky.

"Here he comes."□

The smallest pirate Zeppelin, lit from within like an elongated white lantern, floated toward the parade route.□Naivos' guards looked up impassively as her vehicle slowed, then came to a complete stop. Naivos stood up from her throne, gesticulating angrily. The loudspeaker went silent, and the crowd settled in to watch. As the Zeppelin grew near, a woman in a black cat suit exited the vehicle's undercarriage. The four guards turned and melted into the crowd. People whooped and applauded. Naivos looked around wildly, her face a mask of rage.

Deuce's Zeppelin hovered just above the crowd. A pair of rope ladders appeared, then two men climbed down with practiced grace. Daredevils, Vole thought.□ They reached out with their hands as Naivos tried to scramble away, but the crowd pushed in, lifting her parade float off the ground. There was no escape. The Daredevils reached down and lifted her into the air.□

Over the noise of laughter and music, Forum Representative Natova Naivos screamed. As she was hauled up into the Zeppelin's gondola, the crowd broke into applause. The parade continued as the majestic airship floated up and away.

Chapter Twenty-Two

Migration

As always, Satellite G-24-N7B8 displayed the small, octagonal area on Bilioth, (otherwise known as Authority Planet Designate 19805) where its human population lived. On the night of Solstice, it glowed like an ornament, the ring road surrounded by patches of brightness, dark in the center so the whole thing looked like an old Earthen pastry,□*donut*. The only other significant luminosity was□from the space port to the south.□It was from this small light spur that galactic craft began to ascend, one by one, like bubbles surfacing through the atmosphere.□□

At the same moment, The Vortex Park Medotel had begun to deal with the night's anticipated emergencies; drug reactions, broken bones, and various vehicular accidents. Staff were prepared for the rush. Solstice was their busiest night of the year. After the parade would come worse cases; trauma, concussions, and overdoses. The Medotel was stocked, staffed, and ready. Every Medic in the diaspora knew that this night they could pick up a short, eventful moonlighting job. When the Fest was over, they would get a fat credit transmission and a few days of rest on the pleasure planet. Rumors abounded that

Lafford was overrun with a terrible STD. But on Bilioth, the Medotel was as clean and efficient as a Terminus, and almost as quiet.□

When a small team of Daredevils, led by a young woman in a red Mohawk, appeared in reception and insisted on seeing the Medic in charge, no one knew quite what to make of it. A show of hands selected Medic Penilla Han, a woman of 60 standard years who had seen lots of situations in the war and was known to be good with crazies. But the red-haired girl wasn't in the throes of a psychotic break; within two minutes of her warning, the Playplex lost power. Several staff recognized their visitor as a patient who had been discharged less than two days before, named Minna Tegg. She had stolen Grigg Vidsonnen's Leona, which many considered to be a sign of good sense, not the other way around.

The Medotel switched to auxiliary sources, smoothly and without loss of function. Minna Tegg then announced that every Medic in the building, and all the MedGens, human and Vel.2, should plan to spend the rest of their time on Bilioth working, night and day. Medic Han began trying to examine the girl, insisting that she remain calm until a sedative could be prepared. The four Daredevils in the waiting area started to argue.□

A tall, dark-haired man and a small, well-coiffed woman came in from the street and introduced themselves to Medic Han.□ After a short conversation the three went into former Director Vidsonnen's office. When they emerged fifteen minutes later, Medic Han called a staff meeting, where she instructed all personnel to locate and boot up any and all MedGens.□

Medic Han said, "We have polymers to spin. A lot of them. Station Lafford needs our help, and we are going to give it.

Jauhuaa was passing over the Playplex, when suddenly the false star field below her blinked out. The restful darkness held shapes of white Zeppelins, colorful tiny lanterns, and bonfires, but none of the annoying, jagged rays that sometimes ruined the night. She trimmed her wings to the east, catching a downdraft. It was an important night for the Jaisenets. They were to leave their nesting ground for a season in the tundra outside the fire mountains.□

Jauhuaa could confirm that conditions for their move were favorable.

The gray-braided woman had come to see them, to say goodbye, water streaming from her eyes. One or two of the smallest children had pecked at her face, and she had let them, offering small vegetables to eat, stroking their sides with her flat hands. Jauhuaa hoped she was gone now. She never wanted to see that love-sick old human again. She had forgotten what she was, living with the flock for so long. So had her son. Such confusion was an abomination. Jauhuaa clicked her beak in disgust.

Jauhuaa guessed the younger woman had taken a proper lesson from the Long Wizards, in their wet place. The sudden darkness below made Jauhuaa know that the small human had done something, that her anger after the man was killed, her encounter with the wise people of the cavern, had led to balance, to sanity. Perhaps Jauhuaa's kind would be left in peace.□

She gave a final look behind her. The only lights now were spaceships, rising from the airfield, burning through the high sky like the humans' exploding stars.

The feed from Satellite G-24-N7B8 disappeared at precisely 1 1:42.37 standard time. So did the feed from all the other satellites orbiting Bilioth, with the exception of one; the Authority Interface

Link. It soon filled with data, transmitted to every station, terminus, colony, and settlement in the diaspora. Records, surveillance, maps, traffic patterns, historical information; within a day, every collection of people, however minor, received the same highly classified data set.□

On Forum Station, an emergency meeting of the Law Enforcement Committee was called to discuss what to do when the perpetrator of this data-hoarding crime was eventually caught and prosecuted. By morning, the members still had not decided whether they would call for the death penalty.□

At dawn, a Zeppelin touched down at the Pirate base several hundred klicks away from the Playplex. Two people led the air ship into its hangar, where it parked, and its crew disembarked.

Quaid was exhausted from the many complicated operations he'd set in motion. His people were hosting the past AUD Champions that evening, but he hoped to get a few hours of sleep beforehand. He still couldn't believe Oli wasn't going to be there, except that the last time he'd seen his friend, the man had looked awful. Rumor was, he'd died in deep space, and they'd jettisoned his body. But Quaid didn't put much stock in rumors. He wouldn't be surprised if Oli wasn't really dead at all and showed up that night asking for a stiff drink.

Their guest of honor, Madame Naivos—who had been dragged on board screaming and swearing worse than any Freighter Quaid had ever heard—was peacefully sleeping. After they had explained to her what she was expected to do in return for not being turned over to the authorities, and the old lady had turned over several data drives cleverly hidden in the links of her silver necklace, Nyppio's Medics had injected her with something that looked like water. But it must not have been, because no one had been able to rouse the old lady since. She lay in one of the state rooms, laughing in her sleep, talking nonsense to herself. Quaid figured she'd wake up later that morning.□

That evening, when the Intergalactic Society for Daredevilry had assembled, caught up on gossip, but had not yet started the real drinking and bragging, Quaid would announce the presentation. He needed to refine it, but his rising sense of excitement offered a wealth of enticing ideas. While his pilots had been evading the Jaisenet's migration patterns, which had not been easy, the colorful creatures seemed to be all over the sky that night. Quaid had sat with Nyppio and poured over the data sets that the Freighters had streamed over the diaspora.□

It would take years to sift through all the information. Most of it was junk, and all of it was private, and it felt awkward to look at it. But when you got past that, the hoard represented an enormous opportunity. Nyppio and his friends had pitched this idea, an insane quest, really, that had gnawed at Quaid like a hungry dog from the moment they proposed it.

Like every other time he'd gone off to try something disruptive and foolish, Quaid's gut roiled with emotion. It was dangerous, what they wanted to do. It would take every ounce of ingenuity and courage humans had. But if there was one thing he'd learned on Bilioth, since the early days when there had been nothing there but a blank desert, it was this—tell human beings they can't have something good, then prepare to see just how hard they are willing to go to get it.□

In the data, deep down under restricted folders and dry-looking satellite reports, they had found information so enticing, so intriguing...oh hell. Quaid stopped kidding himself. He wasn't going to get any sleep, not that day, probably not that night, either.

Once he'd seen how few Vel.1s really operated on Earth, how low their energy reserves were, what weak defensive arrays they had, he had jumped on the idea. Velraens were machines. If you sold them an Armistice, as the humans had, apparently, they didn't have the imagination to prepare for that deal to be broken. The Vel.1s who had taken Earth for themselves were sitting ducks.□

The planet itself was a junk pile; infrastructure going back to nature, megafauna multiplying, unexploded ordinance littering both land and sea. The amount of sheer hard work needed to decontaminate and reconstruct the place would be almost unimaginable.

Nah. Taking back Earth wouldn't be easy. If it were, Quaid wouldn't be feeling this way, this combination of stirred and terrified, which signaled the start of the next great adventure. He missed Oli, his oldest and best friend, who would have understood in his very bones, how irresistible was the challenge.□

Quaid said a warrior's prayer just in case his friend really was dead, then went to his private quarters. Like everything else at the base, they were powered by volcano. He fired up his Interface. His presentation didn't have to be detailed. It just needed to transmit a tiny fraction of that passion that every Biliothist intuitively understood, that flame of need, to go out there, and test their limits.□

Quaid would probably die in the attempt, a lot of people would.□*But what a way to go. Epic, legendary...worthy of the attempt.*□The pirate□scratched his red beard and smiled.□

Chapter Twenty-Three

Paradise

V ole and Xan had never hoped to share a dwelling, much less move into a place as sleek and spacious as the apartment Grigg Vidsonnen left behind. They had their pick of Playplex apartments, of course, when the Authority took it upon themselves to remember the regulations disallowing colonies on protected planets.□

Once Bilioth emptied out, only Command employees and a handful of necessary licensees got to stay, as a remote settlement space travelers could limp into if they were sick or having mechanical trouble. Naturally, there had to be some Medics.□

Vidsonnen's place, beautiful and restful as it was, might have been their once-a-week house. But they loved it too much to stray, the grand penthouse and its staff of three Vel.2s. The Aizmirsts filled the once-bachelor pad with their own quiet presence, with MedGens and test tubes and vials of liquid, until the all-white, tasteful suite of rooms took on a lab-like, utilitarian flair that suited the Medics□just fine. Vidsonnen, a person with an active social life, had brought in a bed so large and fine that when there were no cases in the Medotel, Vole might spend a whole day in it. Xan loved those hours the most, looking out at the park from the bank of picture windows, talking, laughing, and making love. Science was important, but not as pressing as making up for lost years.

Soon after Command showed up to enforce the newly remembered regulations, the starships that had sat inert on the red dirt while the Playplex grew up around them fired up their engines and went back into Space from whence they'd come. The process took about a standard year, which was impressive, since a lot of the ships needed to be cleansed of microscopic, pink particles and hallucinogenic spores.□

Once word got out that a mercenary army was massing to take back Earth, every Daredevil or Pirate felt an overwhelming urge to head out to the Cradle Quadrant. No one wanted to miss the most exciting missions or lose out on a chance to gobble up the property they were about to liberate from the Vel.1s. The Freighters Guild had more work than they knew what to do with, gearing up for the onslaught. Even Nyppio enjoyed the solidarity with which the Biliothists turned to their next horizon. All over the diaspora, Earth became the next big thing.

By this time, Waystation Lafford had re-opened, its people inoculated, and the last few patients treated. Vole never returned to the clinic, or her small room. One of the Gens put her few possessions into a case, handed it off to a hazel eyed flight attendant, and moved into the apartment herself.□ The man, glad to do a favor for a fellow veteran, delivered the luggage on one of the last shuttle flights from the Waystation to Bilioth. From that moment forward, the shuttle had a new route, Lafford to Mars.

Vole and Xan often greeted duskwind from the waters of the mineral pool. They would watch mist rise from the turquoise waters, stars emerging in the garnet sky, as the frogs started up their important announcements. Xan let his beard grow, much to his wife's amusement.

Vole would say, "now that you have nothing but time, you can't be bothered to shave?"

And he would say, "We don't have all the time in the world. We have Science to do."

And then they would float some more. This was still the Pleasure Planet, after all.□